The Box

☐ The Box

GEORGE BOWERING

Vancouver
New Star Books
2009

NEW STAR BOOKS LTD.
107 – 3477 Commercial Street | Vancouver, BC v5n 4e8   CANADA
1574 Gulf Road, #1517 | Point Roberts, WA 98281   USA
www.NewStarBooks.com | info@NewStarBooks.com

We acknowledge the financial support of the Canada Council, the
Government of Canada through the Book Publishing Industry
Development Program, the British Columbia Arts Council, and
the Government of British Columbia through the Book Publishing
Tax Credit.

Cover by Mutasis.com
Cover photo by Foncie Pulice
Printed and bound in Canada by Gauvin Press
First printing, October 2009

LIBRARY AND ARCHIVES CANADA CATALOGUING IN PUBLICATION

Bowering, George, 1935–
    The box / George Bowering.

Short stories.
ISBN 978-1-55420-045-0

    I. Title.
PS8503.O875B68 2009   C813'.54   C2009–905061–7

For my friend George Stanley, Vancouver writer.

Contents

Acknowledgments

These stories have appeared, sometimes in different shapes, in: *Vancouver Review, Matrix, Sounds Like Canada* (CBC), *dANDelion, Filling Station, The Capilano Review, Dingers,* ed. David McGimpsey (DC Books), *Rampike, Open Letter, Prism International, Ten Canadian Short Plays,* ed. John Stevens (Dell Books).

Thanks, too, to the following individuals and organizations for their courtesy and assistance: Betty Fairbank, Greg Girard, Jeremy M. Jackson, Art Jones, Kit Krieger, Curt Lang, H.W. Roozeboom, Sharla Sava, Wendy Wimmer Schuchart, Maria Steernberg, -and Vancouver Public Library Special Collections.

The Box

☐ A Night Downtown

Years ago, or why don't I just say it, decades ago, I used to spend quite a lot of my time, back when I did not always think of it as my precious time, a lot of my time walking around downtown. As the years went by I was lucky enough to do a lot of walking, I mean a *lot* of walking, in places such as Sydney and Rome and Cape Town. Yeah, a big shot.

Now every time I go downtown by bus instead of in my car, I am taken by changes. What the hell used to be where that women's shoe store is on Robson Street? What was that hotel called in the olden days, when I came downtown to drink beer in hotel pubs?

Years ago. I actually started this little account with "years ago." Years ago I used to hear my uncle Lou say that. He was talking about a time when he used to wear spats. I know. I have seen them in his basement. Saw them decades ago, as a matter of fact.

It's a good thing that cities don't think about time this way. You would hear groans and sighs at every street corner. At the corner of Robson and Howe, for example. That is where I met Eiko. Years ago.

I was doing my usual two things while walking around. One: I was watching a kind of vaporous movie called *My*

Life, the romance of this unknown hero in his late formative years, practising the moves that would lead to his fame. Two: I had to make everything even. If I stepped on a sidewalk crack with my left shoe I had to step on another one with my right shoe. If I put my left hand against a window I had to put my right hand against that window or another one. Sometimes, if I got too engrossed in making things even, I would have to touch right-left after having touched left-right. Then of course, I had touched left-right-right-left, so it became necessary to touch right-left-left-right, to even up the sequence. You see the problem.

Often a sequence of car-touching in traffic would seem undesirable to a driver whose personal details I knew nothing of. He would speed away before I had put my right hand's fingers on the dew of his roof.

This stuff generally happened on Saturday night, when I had little else to do. I could have been at home, a basement suite on higher ground, trying to learn to write left-handed.

Humming, too. I was often humming while gooping around the streets. I still do the humming, though my gooping days are pretty well over, I would say. Would hum a tune from back in my uncle Lou's day, "Sweet Lorraine," for example, or a tune I was making up on the spot. On the corner of Robson and Howe I stopped humming when I saw a slightly overweight Japanese girl pointing her Yashica at me. I knew it was a Yashica right away, because I was and still am a camera person. Figured out it was a Japanese girl, woman, pretty soon after that.

If you know me, you know what I did next. I struck a pose, would have looked serious to some people, comical to others. As soon as I did that she lowered the Yashica. When I then put on the pose that was supposed to look like not putting on a pose, she lifted and I saw the louvers blink. I smiled. She snapped.

She took a step toward me. I took a step toward her. She made a little Japanese bow.

Of course I tried to bow back and looked awkward as an Englishman in a tropical clime.

She put her hand over her mouth and dipped her forehead and giggled about three consonants. Then she was close enough to be heard, and spoke to me.

"I am sorry if I disturb you."

That's right. She said "sorry", no cliché Nipponese accent.

Disturb?

Are you kidding? I hardly ever met anyone interesting on a Saturday night.

"Not a disturb ... no, you don't ... don't sorry, it's perfectly," I replied.

This was a few decades ago, remember, not lately. Nowadays the young Japanese and Korean and Chinese tourists come through town in twos and fours and twelves, smoking long cigarettes and carrying Hello Kitty bags and wearing pink Yankees caps.

A few decades ago, say fifteen years after the firestorm of Tokyo, they were few, they did not wear designer items, and they did not speak English with just a trace of an accent.

She giggled again, at my discomposure.

"My name is Roger," I told her, picking one from my own family.

"I am Eiko," she said, and lowered her forehead, and raised her eyelids. Her eyes were the only really beautiful part of her.

It was a lovely September night, no rainslick, no wind, the leaves still on the little trees in their concrete tubs along the sidewalk in front of the courthouse. Just that morning I had read the first pages of a novel by Joseph Conrad. I knew the importance of a leafy environment.

"I will make a deal," I told her, while I held the door of the coffee place open. "I will let you take pictures of me if you will tell me what it is about Japanese people and cameras."

She took a picture of me while I was approaching with two

cups of coffee and wondering why she wasn't drinking tea, and when she pointed the business end of her single lens reflex at me, a couple people got behind me to get immortalized, and a couple other people got out of the way, more noisily. And it wasn't even really *that* part of downtown.

I always did a version of that sort of thing. When I saw some people standing in a group to get photographed, I would join them. Who is that guy, I imagined people back in Omaha saying.

Now when we sat in the unpleasant light of the coffee place I could get a good look at her. I could look her over. I averted my eyes every time I caught a glimpse of her. But there she was, an overweight young woman with a haircut that looked like a black beret, glasses that might have been ordered by the gross for a military group, and not anywhere enough of a chin. As she walked into the coffee place I noticed and filed away my very first sight of a woman who was both overweight and bowlegged.

Her voice was no help.

"No accent," she said, and it sounded a little like a parrot trying to sound older, "because I was born in Honolulu. I went to Japan when I was a talking girl, and not voluntarily."

"The US government sent you because of Pearl Harbor."

"No, my parents made me go. The US government made *them* go."

"It could have been worse. You could have been in a concentration camp in California."

"I was in a concentration camp in Japan. Do you think they were glad to see us Americans show up in 1942?"

She gestured, and we up and left the coffee place. Pretty soon we were walking along Granville Street under the neon, and she was unselfconsciously snapping the Yashica at me while I alternately posed like some minor-league Gene Kelly, or affected a casual attitude, seeming to ignore the camera's kazamming shutter.

We managed to talk as if we knew each other, while making our way among the many walking strangers, until we were on the bridge, Chevrolets zipping by. I stopped in at the halfway point and leaned on the rail.

"Japanese tourists and their cameras," I repeated.

She got busy changing the film in her camera. She was so short that she had to reach up to put her stuff on the railing. I wished that she wouldn't do that, but it wasn't my camera or girl or business. I was just a romantic tough guy in the early autumn darkness.

"So, spit it out, Doll," I said.

"Banff. Niagara Falls. More and more Japanese tourists. You will see, one day," she said. Her glasses reflected the bridge light we were under. "But the Japanese."

"Spill it, Sister."

"Japanese people, they have not been to Niagara Falls until they get back home and look at the pictures. There we are in front of the Horseshit Fall."

"Shoe. Falls."

"Okay. Oh, do you mind?"

She asked this of a romantic young couple who were leaning on each other's shoulders as they walked across the bridge.

Sure, why not? Eiko and I were the romantic couple now, standing at the suicide rail of the Granville Street Bridge, sunset a slit by now, but the flash —

"One more, prease," said Eiko.

— caught us surrounded by gloom, and I waited till the real romantic couple had passed out of hearing.

"Prease?"

"People like to hold on to their illusions about the exotic East," she said.

Damn. I actually took her hand as we walked across the bridge, I mean not to the other end, but to the other side, and started walking back into downtown. Some kind of vessel with a two-stroke engine chugged out of False Creek below us. A guy on a bicycle cursed us as he barely flitted between us and the car traffic to our left.

Under the covers in her plain hotel room, I forgot how short and plain and bowlegged she looked, and enjoyed the soft curves of a slightly overweight female human being. She rubbed me in a way that was entirely new to me, and showed me that smart as I thought myself to be, there had been a lot I did not know until an hour ago.

Here is where I usually liked to have a cigarette or a nap, but my eyes were wide open in the way that an oyster is wide open after being shucked by a hungry expert. Red and green lights made their way along the edges of the window curtain. Eiko's camera was on the little plywood desk, its eye aimed at us, but it remained silent. I had a heretofore unknown taste in my mouth.

"Eiko? What does it mean?" I asked, after clearing my throat twice.

"It is a girl's name," she said.

"That's it? I thought that in Japan girls' names were the names of flowers and things."

"Some of them are. Not mine. There goes one of your illusions about the exotic East."

"I gladly exchange it for the new things I am learning about the exotic East. No one has ever told me about that thing you did with the string of pearls."

I grinned in the red light and the green light.

I touched her nearest curve with my left hand. Then I rolled just the littlest bit and touched it with my right hand.

"I'm still here, Roger," she said.

I wondered whether the dim-coloured light improved my looks as much as it did hers.

"I have a dumb occidental question to ask you," I said, settling with my left hand. "Referring to that business about Japanese tourists and how they have not really been to, say, the Vatican until they get their Vatican pictures back."

"Mmm, I know approximately what you are going to ask," she said in a kind of whisper, lovely. She touched me with some fingernails, I don't know which.

Physicist P.A.M. Dirac suggested that experimental confirmation is not necessary for a truly elegant theory. Did you know that?

"Yes, of course it has to do with that stuff about you Japanese tourists and your cameras and reality and that. If the reality comes into being when you are at home showing your prints or slides, wouldn't it have been enough just to have *pictures* of me?"

"Think about it, Vancouver person," she said, and put a kiss on the end of my nose, off of which the perspiration had just dried. "The picture of the young Japanese girl standing in front of Niagara Falls proves that she was actually there at last."

"At last."

"Yes, in the sense that at last we have the picture. But here ," she said, pointing her short finger at the Yashica, "I have only the proof that I have been on some street beside you."

Green red green red.

"Not necessarily a love affair," I said, trying to sound thoughtful. "That gizmo wasn't taking pictures while we were — ?"

Little Japanese giggle.

"No. We may be noisy people, but we would have heard that Yashica shutter."

"So," I said, my post-prandial brain trying to kick into operation, "what proof are you going to have that you had a fling with a — what am I called?"

"Hakujin."

"Gesundheit."

"What proof have you got that you had a fling with a tourist from Japan?" she asked, and she reached for her socks.

"I, I, I don't need proof. I have my memory. Very nice memory," I said, and she opened the blind. Her short wide bare-naked body was red and green.

"Come on. I will walk you to your bus. Maybe take one last picture of you."

"Last? You're going home?"

"Pants on, Canadian boy."

We were not holding hands when we started along the sidewalk. Traffic was pretty heavy, and there were plenty of people along Granville. A young woman wearing a white parka and a camera around her neck smiled at us. She had dull white skin and very big blue eyes.

This woman spoke as we met and passed.

"Karen, you're the best," she said.

☐ An Experimental Story

1. Introduction and hypothesis.

It is a commonly held belief that an innocent country boy or girl, upon moving to the city, will be exposed to temptations great in number and strong in attraction, that his or her innocence will be attacked, and in most cases, at least bruised, if not entirely battered. He or she may be debauched or hardened or criminalized or even robbed of life. Less has been said about the youth who moves from the iniquitous city to a bucolic setting. Even Émile Zola, our great founder of experimental fiction, never investigated such an eventuality.

I am a city dweller who spent his boyhood in the orchard country of south-central British Columbia. Though I have often heard people point out that I retain some of my early innocence, I also know something of the darker corners in metropolitan life, far from my mother's eye. My best friend moved from the city to my village when we were about ten, so I did not look to him for my information, although a psychologist might.

It seemed to me unlikely that a youth who has been on the relevant streets long enough to be somewhat corrupted would revert to a natural innocence upon moving to the sticks. I thought we could postulate that it was unlikely that he or she would remain at a constant level, juvenile subjectivity being as precarious as it is alleged to be. And although we should remain scientifically open to data so as not to discount the possibility out of hand that the city youth would become tainted by rural life, I was of the opinion that this outcome was least likely.

It was my hypothesis that we could expect results somewhere in the middle of the range I have described. I thought that a street-wise Vancouver youth would, after interacting with the natural setting, the social tapestry and the native individuals of the south Okanagan Valley, begin to develop characteristics that would make him resemble Huckleberry Finn more than Studs Lonigan, to use a couple of standards set in an earlier time in the United States.

2. Materials.

I thought for some time before I decided to select a boy rather than a girl, and rather than a number of boys or girls or both. I found a fourteen-year-old white boy with an English last name who was living on West 14th Avenue near Oak Street in Vancouver, a gentle flat area not far from Vancouver General Hospital, where his mother, a single parent from the word *go*, was a nurse in the maternity ward. She just plain grew tired of living in the city where you can not find a parking spot, and the bus never comes, and accepted a position at the Royal South Okanagan Hospital in Lawrence, one of the smaller towns in the valley.

The boy's name was Drew, as were about 20 percent of the boys in his classrooms at school. He was between grades nine and ten when he and his mother moved into a two-bedroom house within walking distance of the high school. Drew had never lived in a house, and the prospect did something to alleviate his unhappiness at leaving his companions behind. He also felt a little better when he saw that the boys here in the sticks wore the same outfits as did the boys at his old school. They were just as eager as he was to wear things with the most popular brand names and logos on them. They wore long silky basketball shorts and huge sports shoes made by children their age in Asian factories.

Drew had been masturbating regularly for a year and a half, and had once placed his hand on the warmer part of a girl's thigh, but most of his sexual experience came via the Internet. He did not know that his mother, who shared the computer, could click some square and see a list of the internet sites he had visited lately.

So he was not really a debauchee, just a city kid with dirty notions. As to other measurements of innocence, well, he and his companions, or his "homies," as he liked to call them, boosted stuff at Chinese corner stores, entering as a group of four, say, and scattering around so that the owner's teenage son at the front till could not watch them all at once. The same guys would open the door of any parked car that was not locked, and gather change or CDs or items of clothing. They would throw most of the items of clothing under a hedge, and if the CD turned out to be Mozart or Dwight Yoakam, it would go sailing onto someone's roof.

I don't know whether you would call that a disappearance of innocence. I would call it stupidity, myself.

So this youth from the Coast was the material that I found myself focusing on the most, but of course the village of Lawrence was pretty important in itself. Any experiment features the introduction of some material into a material that it has till then been unconnected with.

The nature of the valley is pretty well known to anyone who has read any of those magazines that they throw onto your front porch in the western half of Vancouver. Vineyards stretch green along the formerly light brown benches of the valley's hills, and whatever orchards remain range along both sides of little Highway 97, which has been getting more and more secondary since Highway 97A was put in a few decades ago to zip travellers from the Kootenays to the Coast. More than half the trees bear apples, and the rest sport, in order of their picking seasons, cherries, apricots, peaches, pears, plums and prunes, as well as a few other fruits that are more for family interest than for commercial use.

Orchardists have always been put-upon people, beset by bad weather and a paucity of sudden seasonal workers. In latter times they have had to keep up with fickle tastes on the part of the consumers, as they had come to be called. Old time varieties of apples, Winesaps and Newtons, for example, had to be rooted out and replaced by Galas and Braeburns or something like that. The tall trees that had once been negotiated with 24-foot ladders, had to be yanked out and replaced by small trees close together, reachable by an average-sized itinerant labourer from Quebec.

When Drew and his mother moved into the valley, it was pear and prune season. When Drew's mother first heard about this, she complained that someone must have got it wrong. Prunes, she said, are dried plums. Old people eat them or drink their juice in order to regularize their excretion. She is a nurse, after all, so her son nearly avoided this argument. But he was a teenager.

"Well, I have a job starting tomorrow," said Drew, "and I am supposed to be picking prunes. Drew Bartkowski told me that prunes are just about the easiest thing to pick, because the trees are low and there are tons of prunes on every branch, and you take them all off. With peaches you have to go over the tree three or four times, apparently."

His mother was astonished. It had been a long time since she had heard him say three sentences in a row.

"Plums," she replied. "You will probably be picking plums."

"Drew said prunes, and he lives here."

"So do we," said his mother. "Well, a job. Now, let's see — what will you need?"

"Sunblock and a lunch," said Drew.

3. *Procedure.*

Mrs. Van Hoorn had a five-acre orchard up behind the little air strip, and it was pretty evenly divided between cherries and Italian prunes, a rather unusual combination in this part of the country. She had the good old fashioned giant Bing cherry trees, now offering only leaves and hardened sap along old wounds in their trunks. The prune trees were short, and could be handed easily with a ten-foot ladder.

Drew had told her up front that he was new to this kind of work, but she said that Paddy would show him how it's done. Work starts at 8:00 and goes to 5:00, she said, with half an hour for lunch and two breaks. He got the idea that Paddy was not a relative, but some kind of old friend, or uncle, or employee from an earlier time. There did not seem to be any Mr. Van Hoorn, or at least if there was, he was somewhere else.

Most of the orchard women around here would be up in a tree picking, or driving the tractor around, but Mrs. Van Hoorn did not do that sort of thing. She was a painter, she said, and worked on the shaded patio of her little square stucco house in the middle of the orchard, or inside the house itself. She left Drew to Paddy, who had thick curly white hair that he did not put a hat on despite the desert sun, and a pipe that was always in his mouth, sometimes with the bowl upside down.

He showed Drew how to move his ladder in the high grass, where to hang his picking pail. Mainly he showed him how to handle the fruit. He said that you should not yank the prunes off the branch, but lift them off backward. It's the same with everything, cherries, pears and all. And don't drop them into the pail. You don't want to handle fruit the way you see guys throwing it into bins at the supermarket in Vancouver.

"You want to hold it gently, as if it was your girlfriend's tit."

Drew didn't have a girlfriend, but he felt his face going red anyway. He had just a minute ago been thinking of Mrs. Van Hoorn's tits. He had once heard the word *breasts*, and thought it was the most embarrassing word ever.

While Drew picked his pail full and carefully emptied it into the boxes and moved his ladder, he felt the hot sun on his sunblocked neck. Pretty soon he said to hell with it and took off his shirt and hung it on a low branch that had no more prunes on it. But now his white west-coast back was bared to the sun, and by later afternoon it was forty degrees in the shade and he was not in the shade all that often.

He managed to rub sunblock on the backs of his shoulders all right, and got a little, awkwardly, around the side of his rib cage, but he could already feel the burning air in the middle of his back. He couldn't ask Paddy to rub it on, could he, Paddy, who didn't wear a hat. Drew was wearing a green baseball cap with some incomprehensible skateboard logo on the front.

By lunch time he was already pink and red all over his back. Sweat was running down his legs, and he decided that tomorrow he would wear shorts instead of jeans, and he would sunblock his legs. He sat down on the trailer that was hooked to Mrs. Van Hoorn's little tractor, and looked at the pitiful little stack of prune boxes he had filled. Paddy had filled four for each one he had managed, and Paddy's boxes did not have leaves mixed in with the purple fruit. He smelled the tobacco from Paddy's pipe, and contemplated bringing cigarettes tomorrow.

Mrs. Van Hoorn came out with a jug of ginger beer and two tall plastic cups. Drew sniffed at the liquid in his cup.

"Best thing in the world for this climate," said Paddy in an accent that may have been Irish and may just have been old-timer. "That and salt tablets. I never bother with the salt tablets, but there's them that does."

Mrs. Van Hoorn was wearing old-fashioned white pleated tennis shorts and a man's shirt. There was a streak of blue paint on the outer side of one thigh. She had put the jug down on the trailer beside Drew, and was turning to head back to the house, when she stopped and looked at him.

"You are going to have a bad burn on that back. It's going to peel something awful. You should have sunblock on it," she said.

"I can't reach," he said, and he had not started eating his sandwich.

"Well, you have to have some protection. The sun in this part of the country is nothing to joke about."

And she spied his tube of sunblock in the grass below his shirt. When she bent to pick it up, Drew felt that he should be looking elsewhere, but he was not fast enough. Then she was squeezing a big gob of sunblock cream onto the palm of her hand. She rubbed her palms together and approached him.

"Give me your back," she said.

He could not speak, really, but he managed a kind of throat sound with his mouth closed. Then he felt her hands on his back. They were strong and unhesitating. It must be because she is an artist, he thought. He felt like a piece of art. He didn't know what he was feeling. Her hands moved all over his back, from the back of his neck to just a little in at the top of his jeans. Her hands seemed to go on forever, for a long time, anyway. She lives in the Okanagan Valley. She understands how to do this sunblock business. He felt her hands on the sides of his waist, and the fingers went just a little around front.

He was going to have to sit here for a while. There was no chance of standing up, not just now. Paddy was nowhere in sight.

"There you go," she said, and she was walking back to the house, holding her hands in the air in front of her.

4. *Quantitative Data.*

Number of flats or boxes of prunes picked by Drew between 8:00 a.m. and 5:00 p.m. on his first day: 19.

Number picked by Paddy: 79.

Minimum temperature between 8:00 a.m. and 5:00 p.m.: 18°C.

Maximum temperature between 8:00 a.m. and 5:00 p.m.: 41°C.

Number of prunes eaten by Drew between 8:00 a.m. and noon: 21.

Number of prunes eaten by Drew between 1:00 p.m. and 5:00 p.m.: 1.

Number of erections experienced by Drew before noon: 4.

Number of erections experienced by Drew after noon: 22.

Number of erections experienced by Paddy: none.

We should factor in a chance of error in this compilation, of perhaps plus or minus two erections for Drew, the count becoming questionable, as I myself had at least one and perhaps two while thinking of Mrs. Van Hoorn. This occurred by accident as my mind drifted away from the scene in the orchard and over to and inside the little stuccoed and vine-covered house, where it was cooler than it was in the sunlight, but still warm enough to induce the shedding of some clothing, as for instance by Mrs. Van Hoorn, who was unbuttoning her shirt and moving her shoulders to get free of it, until she wore nothing but the tennis shorts and one of those scalloped bras that do not enclose the breasts (there's that word) so much as they hold them up a little from underneath. Mrs. Van Hoorn, being of average height, stood on a chair and raised herself upon her tiptoes to bring down the curtain rod for the living room window. It was, I suppose, time to wash that off-white curtain.

It was Heisenberg, wasn't it, who proclaimed that during a scientific observation, the observer affects the experiment in observing it. In the sharp formulation of the law of causality — "if we know the present exactly, we can calculate the future" — it is not the conclusion that is wrong but the premise. The path comes into existence only when we observe it.

Cause and effect was such a revolutionary idea when the scientists and then the medical doctors and then Émile Zola got a hold of it. Then along came those white pleated tennis shorts. They were old-fashioned — that means that they had buttons rather than a zipper.

All right — we are doing Quantitative Data. There were four white buttons.

5. Qualitative Data.

There are, in all experiments that involve human subjects, or even subjects from the animal kingdom, except for, perhaps, insects and fish, certain data that cannot be quantified, even data that is unexpected. Having placed a city boy in an orchard just outside a little town in the August heat, we realize that our desire to see whether he becomes more innocent, or stays about the same, or somehow continues his path away from the "visionary gleam" is not going to be satisfied quickly. We know that we are but beginning a long process of observation, and that many laboratory reports such as this one will have to be piled up before we can venture any thorough conclusion.

A lot depends, for example, on the nature of desert sunlight between the branches of fruit trees. Drew had not brought his sunglasses, or "shades" as he and his "homies" called them. They would have made things only more difficult in the cool dark under the laden trees. But if you look up at a wall of white stucco blasted by white sun, you will not truly be seeing, but only shone upon. If you see a window in that wall, it will appear as a square of blackness. In that square of blackness, Drew saw a little bit of white rise and stay and descend. This white was Mrs. Van Hoorn's tennis shorts.

Drew did not know that. He was standing on the fourth step of his ladder and picking prunes without thinking about them. What he saw was folded into his imagination, which a moment earlier had displayed his rising and rising from the polished floor and jamming a basketball, one-handedly, into the middle of a hoop that it was hard to believe had exactly twice the diameter of a basketball.

The white blur was an egret rising silently and skating away in the south wind.

Drew stopped, three prunes in his right hand, and stared at the black rectangle on the white glare. The egret did not reappear. Nor did anything else. He returned to the world of boxes and grass and pails and trees. This was a work space. For a lot of people it, or something like it, would be a piece of calendar art, a dream of Eden, what I did on my summer holidays. I have a job, he had told his mother, and it was the first time he had ever done such a thing on his own. This might not be the onset of adulthood, but it was definitely the goodbye to childhood.

This was a conclusion he was led to during the afternoon appearance of the ginger beer. Mrs. Van Hoorn was barefoot in the dust, and she was wearing the white shorts and a halter top, a bright parrot-patterned piece of cloth with an extravagant bow tied in back. When she put the jug and glasses down on the trailer bed, Drew was going to look away, polite boy that he was, but something made him remain attentive and he saw a bead of perspiration descend between her tanned breasts, and disappear. There was also perspiration in the hair combed back above her ears, and that too was something to see.

He didn't know it but he was beginning to conclude that that was it for childhood. He drank the ginger beer, and told Paddy that he had never tasted it before.

"Aye, boy," said the white-haired man. "At your age you will be tasting a lot of things for the first time."

The remark was of such an obvious nature that even Drew got an inkling of what Paddy was saying through him to the owner of this fruit ranch.

Or he may have just been a hoping boy, hoping for something he really knew nothing about. That would be my interpretation of qualitative data, anyway.

One tug, the boy thought, as he watched Mrs. Van Hoorn walk barefoot and carefully back up the slight grade to her house.

Readers of my report might be somewhat skeptical regarding my observations, especially as they would seem to be made from the point of view of my subject, young Drew. One could argue, though I admit faultily, that as quantitative data would seem to be objective, so qualitative data would appear subjective. That is not going to be my tack, as I have recently done some light reading about the theoretical and experimental work of Werner Heisenberg.

All I will tell you is that I used to be fourteen years old, and when I was fourteen years old I worked in more than one orchard in the south Okanagan Valley. If you think that that disqualifies or disquantifies me as an observer, I will say that this is a post-Heisenbergian experiment. It is careful as can be, nevertheless.

I can tell you, for example, that young Drew had a stomach ache for about an hour in the later part of the afternoon. It would be reasonable to surmise that the cause was the unusual number of prunes he had eaten during the forenoon. When he went to have a pee behind a distant tree, he paused in his walking for a few seconds while the ache tapered off a bit.

Drew liked to read a moderate number of books and magazines, but he was not a boy to analyze over much regarding what he had read and how he saw his position in the world. Thus he did not, not even fleetingly, compare himself to

Adam in the Garden. Thoughts of innocence and its loss did not approach him. Perhaps it was a Creator that was missing from the scenario.

The city is west of there, anyway.

6.Calculations.

On his first day on the job the youngster from the Coast picked 19 boxes of Italian prunes. Each box weighs 24 pounds net. (The box size was created before Canada's adoption of worldwide measurements.) That means that he picked 456 pounds of prunes. As he was being paid 10.5 cents per pound, he earned $47.88 for a first day's pay. He started at 8:00 a.m. and finished at 5:00 p.m., with a half hour for lunch and two fifteen-minute breaks for ginger beer. So his hourly wage for that first day amounted to $5.98 and a sliver an hour. Back on the Coast he could have made about that much for cleaning smears off tables in a hamburger joint.

He had been in a lot of those hamburger joints, pizza joints, chicken joints, and he had never seen anyone like Mrs. Van Hoorn running any of them. I am not saying that that is an observation that belongs in "Calculations," but it did come to mind, his and mine.

The conclusion we want to come to, remember, has something to do with the change in innocence and behaviour that may be observed when a subject is moved from an urban environment to a rural one. The trick is to organize one's data and make one's calculations and remain clear of any undue attention to ephemeral facts or images.

All right. Paddy smoked tobacco twelve times during the working day. Drew did not use any tobacco except some second-hand smoke, which was not unpleasant, Paddy favouring a sweet mixture with a trace of cypress.

Drew was not lazy. Nor was he greedy. He was about as good a worker as you could expect given his age and experience and place of origin. That is what Paddy thought, in any case. The boy may have been momentarily guilty of some vice of which an observer might not be aware, such as avarice, or lust. Well, there was the beer, but surely that might be set down to usage and tradition sooner than to vice.

Mrs. Van Hoorn brought out the beer, three bottles of Kokanee, with heavy dew on the outside of the brown glass, just as she had twice brought out the ginger beer. This time, though, there was no pitcher to empty into the glasses. She did the pouring in the shade of a prune tree that had been picked that day. There were leaves on the trampled grass under the tree. The beer made nice foam that almost spilled over the rim of the glass that Drew was holding, his long day's work done. Unlike ginger beer, Kokanee was something that he had tasted before, though he had never had one poured for him by an adult person.

He kind of liked the flavour, or as they call it in beer circles, the taste. He watched Paddy to see how fast you were supposed to drink it, but Paddy had his pocket knife out and was carving the plug out of the bowl of his pipe. Mrs. Van Hoorn took a moderate sip and looked at him over the rim of her glass, upon which the sun, still pretty high in the sky at the end of the workday, glistened enough to make things disappear from sight.

Drew had had a beer before, as I mentioned, or rather he had shared a beer or two from time to time, on those nights when he stayed later than usual at a friend's place and there was beer in the fridge, or someone brought a bottle or two to the beach. This was his first daylight beer, and there was an understanding that it was meant to put something back into his body that had been expended in a hard day's work under the hot sun. He had his shirt back on now, but he could feel the sweat in it. It would be impossible to calculate the amount of stuff that had come out of him, and though it might be possible to measure the 375 ml that were entering his stomach and so on, there was no way of figuring out how much necessary stuff he was replenishing himself with.

Before he knew it his glass and his bottle were empty and foam stains were disappearing. Now he would jump on his mountain bike and head for home, where his mother would have pasta and salad and milk ready and would be too busy to smell his breath.

So he calculated.

Mrs. Van Hoorn's halter top was securely tied, it would appear. When she got up to gather the bottles and glasses, her breasts swung inside the cloth a little. Drew felt as if he should be apologetic for something. He remembered to pick up his lunch kit and walked two rows over to his bike. Here in the country, his mother had not yet nagged him to wear his helmet.

7. *Results.*

"What do you think?" asked Paddy. "Will this one be a sticker?"

"I expect we'll see him at 8:00 tomorrow," said Mrs. Van Hoorn.

"How was the first day on the job?" asked his mother. She was still wearing her string-tied white sports trousers and discount sports shoes from work.

"I can handle it," he replied.

She thought of that as a pretty good start. He might manage another sentence at dinner. They were going to eat in the back yard, where the television was not a factor.

"Would you like to stay for supper?" asked Mrs. Van Hoorn. "There's corn on the cob."

"Ah, I would," he said. "But I've got a Lodge dinner at the hotel."

"You will probably be a little stiff tomorrow," said his mother, as she used the edge of the big spoon to pull some peas onto his plate.

His lips lifted a little at the edges.

"Oh, I expect so," he said. "From time to time."

Mrs. Van Hoorn was alone now as the sun found its place behind a mountain that always brought an early twilight to this part of the valley, alone except for her large muscular cat to whom she had bequeathed the name "Frankie."

"I believe that I will have one more glass of beer," she told him.

Drew went off to his bedroom earlier than usual. He had to get up early for work.

When she opened his lunch kit to clean it out, she found it almost full of ripe plums.

8. Conclusions.

I understand that any generalization I might make as a result of this experiment will, at best, serve as a hypothesis for another experiment, whether conducted by me or by another observer. I also understand that more than one conclusion might be made following the results seen above.

Did young Drew experience and exhibit any changes regarding his innocence as a result of moving from the west side of Vancouver to Lawrence in the Okanagan? Or were any changes only those that might be expected of a boy that age?

It is my tentative conclusion, if such a phrase be allowed (and why would it not, in a world that hears people talk about "cautious optimism"?), that the climate and weather in the orchard country during autumn served to arouse in Drew's daytime whim and nighttime fancy, thoughts and images that were in an earlier time called "lewd." (And here is another factor prompting relativism: how can we make conclusions concerning innocence and its loss when standards regarding social behaviour have gone through such thorough changes?)

The climate and weather, perhaps as much as the personalities involved, had their effect on attire, perspiration and post-work libation.

On the one hand, the boy, Drew, might be said to have given in to lustful thoughts. But you must also remember that he became an honest worker. I recall a similar balancing-off when I was that age and did the self-examination one might expect in such a reflective youth as I was. What I assume he will assume? Which of us is even now in her dark orchard, trying to get a glimpse of the lighted interior? In any experiment one tries to shine a light there. But I am not here to make conclusions about myself. Or am I? Does Heisenberg reach that far?

☐ Don't Make Him Mad

VOICE: It happens once in a while: a man flies into a rage about something large or puny, and his fit of anger turns into a heart attack before your eyes. His wide-open eyes are the last you see of him alive.

This happened to a lawyer named Brian Nesbitt very early in the twenty-first century, and what a surprise it was to this man of worldly logic to find himself in an unearthly room also occupied by a very large angel with big impressive wings.

If he could have found his voice he would have asked why it was that angels are the only winged creatures who also have arms.

ANGEL: I presume that you will want to argue your own case?

NESBITT: There's a case? What are you talking about?

ANGEL: You stand accused of Wrath, sometimes called Anger. It is one of the seven deadly sins, or as we generally call them, the seven capital vices. I am attorney for the Lord.

NESBITT: Seven deadly sins? That's something from the dark ages. Hell —

ANGEL: (Snickers).

NESBITT: Hell, television commercials are all about the seven deadly sins. They are in favour.

ANGEL: You will have a week to prepare your defence. Or ten years. It's not easy to tell the difference up here.

NESBITT: But Wrath, Anger, it's not a crime. There is no law against it where I come from.

ANGEL: Check it out. None of them are crimes. Sloth, Envy, Avarice. They are character flaws, and the Lord does not like them. You have a week or so.

After what seemed like an eternity, counsellor Nesbitt found himself back in that room. He was carrying a lot of books, and so was the angel.

ANGEL: I defer to the apoplectic gentleman in the nice suit.

NESBITT: I maintain that the case should be thrown out of court, on the grounds that I am not a Catholic. A bunch of rules made up by Saint Gregory the Great and Thomas Aquinas mean nothing to me. I figure the Ten Commandments will do it. They tell a person what not to do.

ANGEL: It matters nothing that you are not a Catholic. Heck, in *Acts* 19 we hear about the wrath of the silversmiths in Ephesus who made a lot of money off their images of Diana. God took care of them.

NESBITT: Yes, with *his* wrath. The whole of the Old Testament is full of the wrath of God. He was always getting really pissed off and smashing whole cities and all. Isn't he setting a rather bad example?

ANGEL: It's too bad you are not a Catholic. You might have read St. Augustine, who points out that God's wrath comes out of his righteousness.

NESBITT: I never yet heard of a person who did not feel righteous when he was flying into a rage.

ANGEL: In any case, you should read St. Augustine. He points out that the New Testament is about replacing wrath with faith.

NESBITT: Sort of a big anger management course?

ANGEL: More like scapegoating. In the olden days the priests would lay all the deadly sins on a goat and send it packing. God's son Jesus is kind of a scapegoat for all our sins, deadly and otherwise.

NESBITT: Well, I remember him getting really mad. Wasn't he guilty of wrath when he went into the temple and turned over the moneychangers' tables and flailed around him with a whip?

ANGEL: Ah, read a little more closely. John says that Jesus made a scourge by knotting a bunch of small cords. Imagine him sitting there tying these knots. You can't do that if you're jumping up and down with rage, eh?

NESBITT: Jesus never got mad? I thought he was supposed to be partly human.

ANGEL: Once. It gets mentioned once, by Mark. He was all set to heal a guy's withered hand, but it was a Sabbath day, and a bunch of right-wingers were looking shocked that he might do some healing on a Sabbath day. Mark says that Jesus felt terribly sad that these right-wingers had such hardened hearts, and he got an angry look in his eyes.

NESBITT: See?

ANGEL: Whose side are you on in that story?

NESBITT: Wait a minute, you're changing the subject —

ANGEL: No, you see, Jesus was also partly God. He was acting out of righteousness.

NESBITT: You can't —

ANGEL: You don't forgive Jesus. He asks God to forgive you. If you have faith in that, you don't need wrath and God doesn't either.

NESBITT: Shakespeare is always going on about wrath. Malcolm says to Macduff: "Let grief / Convert to anger; blunt not the heart, enrage it."

ANGEL: I am glad you brought up Shakespeare. I knew him, by the way. A gentler, more friendly man you never met. And you will remember that Desdemona says to Othello: "I understand the fury in your words / But not the words."

NESBITT: Well, maybe Othello's tragic flaw wasn't anger. Maybe it was stupidity.

ANGEL: Not a deadly sin, but I see your point. No, all the deadly sins are revolts against God's rule. If you check out man's first disobedience in the Garden of Eden, you will see that the snake tells Eve that the fruit can make gods out of her and her hubby.

NESBITT: That brings up a major point in my defence. Is sin promoted by an outside influence, like a snake, or is it a born inclination? Seems as if I get off on either count.

ANGEL: Boy, St. Augustine would eat you for breakfast. Anyway, the Hebrew word for "revolt" means to be like God. Dangerous idea, sinner.

NESBITT: Yeah? Well, our word "anger" comes from the Old Norse word for sorrow. Sorrow isn't a deadly sin.

ANGEL: Funny you should mention that. It used to be, but the Church fathers took it out and put in sloth.

NESBITT: Oh, that's a good one.

ANGEL: It makes the Protestants happy.

NESBITT: I looked up "wrath," too. It comes from an Old English word for twist, twisted, writhing.

ANGEL: As when you're getting browned off and someone tells you not to get your shirt in a knot.

NESBITT: [Pause] Have you ever noticed that the word "angel" is one last consonant away from the word "anger"?

ANGEL: [Somewhat impatient] Well, and if I add another consonant we get "danger."

VOICE: [From outside] Will you hurry up in there? We have fifteen cases of greed to do today.

ANGEL: [More impatient] Keep your wings on. We're almost done.

VOICE: Well, don't take an eternity.

ANGEL: [Raising his voice] Go have another doughnut, you fat slob.

NESBITT: [Chuckles] You tell him Ainge.

ANGEL: [Shouting] You shut up!

VOICE: Shake a leg in there, will you? Why do you always have to get into some smart-aleck discussion with them?

NESBITT: [Shouts] You butt out! [Laughs]

ANGEL: [Shouting] Both of you shut the hell up!

NESBITT: Ah ha ha ha.

ANGEL: [Really loses it] God damn it!

SOUND: CLAP OF THUNDER. It turns into a HISS OF ELECTRICITY.

☐ The Box

I just checked the date in my diary. It was January 17, 1962, a rainy afternoon at the corner of Granville and Georgia in downtown Vancouver, in case you don't know. Well, not all that stuff was the date. You now have the place and the weather. Roy Harris's eighth symphony premiered in San Francisco later that evening, but this story is not about music. The Beatles' first single had just been released in England, but we don't care about that.

It was a Wednesday afternoon. It was also my best friend Will's twenty-fifth birthday, but he was having sushi with his girlfriend. I was celebrating it all alone. Or I was planning to. I had had one beer and read fifteen pages of Joseph Conrad's *Chance* at the Castle pub, and now I was planning to have another beer at the Georgia, a couple of blocks west. I still have that copy of *Chance*, a beaten cheap semi-hardback published by Methuen and Company that I had got somewhere for ten cents, the kind of bargain I liked back in those days. I probably got it in 1958 in Kamloops.

No, I don't think I was in Kamloops in 1958. I was there on certain occasions from 1954 to 1957, when I was in the air force, and had to take a bus up to Kamloops to catch a train back east when my two-weeks' leave were over. Or, wait, I guess I was in Kamloops in 1958, because after I lost

37

my job up north, I had to hitchhike back down with my
new Paris boots not even scuffed up much, and I think the
longest ride I got was from Prince George to Kamloops. I
don't remember whether I bought a book there, though.

No, wait a minute, that hitchhiking took place in 1954,
just before I joined the air force. In 1958 I was working in
the forestry around Merritt. I might have gone into Kamloops then, or maybe I bought that book for ten cents at
some church sale in Merritt, though as I remember, I was in
pubs a lot more than I was in churches, if indeed I was even
in a church. I do remember two books I read in a tent beside
a lake in the mountains not far from Merritt. The other two
people in my crew were out on the lake fishing, while I was
reading. One of the books was *Turvey* by Earle Birney, and
the other was *The Secret Agent* by Joseph Conrad. So who
knows? Maybe I was on a Conrad kick then.

Oh, and I just now pulled down that copy of *Chance*, and
it has Earle Birney's name written on the inside front cover,
in his hand. And now I just heard Earle Birney's voice on
the radio, though he's been dead for a dozen years. I'd stay
out of this story if I were you.

I didn't read *Chance* till early in 1962. It's funny now to
think of summer 1958, though. There I was beside a lake
in the mountains of British Columbia, while in the mountains of eastern Cuba, Fidel Castro and Camilo Cienfuegos
were gathering an army that was getting bigger and bigger and making Fulgencio Batista and Meyer Lansky think
about getting off the island.

Anyway, there I was, standing on the corner in front of
the Hudson's Bay building, waiting for a light. I wasn't
right exactly on the corner, I mean the curb, because there
was a drizzle. I was standing under the awning or whatever
the protection was called on the Bay building. Years later
you would always see a strange religious guy there, standing behind a hand-painted sign, and holding out a neck-
lace with a cross on it. He was horribly skinny, in really

old clothes, with a scraggly beard all different lengths, and
eyes like pickled eggs.

But he didn't show up till about 1970. I'll tell you who was
there, though. The woman that handed me the package.
That's what this is all about.

Here is where I should be making a description of that
woman, but to tell the truth — and that *is* the idea, isn't
it — I can't remember much about her. Maybe she was a
little older than I, or maybe a little younger, but not much
either way. She was, I suppose, wearing January clothes for
Vancouver, whatever that meant in early 1962. I was just
standing there, as I said, waiting for a light.

"Need a light?" asked this woman, not fat, I would have
remembered that.

The light I had been waiting for was the traffic light, but
I did have a cigarette in my mouth. I smiled and leaned my
head forward as one would do, my right hand up to protect
the little flame from the wind and rain. I took a drag, as we
always used to say, and let out the smoke, and finally said
"Thanks," but she was nowhere in sight.

I had a burning cigarette. It was a Sportsman, I can tell
you that much. And I had a small box in my left hand.

"Hey!"

That's what I said, looking every way and even into the
big store. There were some people there, but none that had
anything to do with my scene. The box in my left hand was
a cube, about six inches, as we said then, in any direction.
It was neither heavy nor light. It was made of some kind of
recently-cut coniferous wood, and tied shut, it appeared,
with butcher string.

You don't remember butcher string, do you? In butcher
shops in those days there was a kind of cone of wrapped
string, brownish, rough, twine, you would call it, hanging
above the butcher's head. He had a stack of slick brown
paper in sheets or he pulled it off a roll, and he would slap
your chop on the paper, or he would use his little wooden

spear and lift the jiggling liver onto this paper, and yank down some twine and tie that meat package up fast. He had a way of breaking that twine that you could never do in your first ten tries.

So there I was, a lit cigarette in my mouth, a book as usual in one hand, and a box in the other. I didn't have an umbrella, so I tucked the box and the book inside my open jacket and caught the light to cross Granville and hike the two blocks to the Georgia. For the first few years in Vancouver, after my stint in the air force, I had refused to go to the Georgia pub, because that was where arty-farty types from the campus paper and the players club went, including a lot of guys with British accents, most of them named Tony. I was a book-reading guy and planned on being a book-writing guy, and that meant reading lots of people such as Conrad and Hardy and Forster, but when I had been a kid in the valley I had resented all the self-important people with British accents. I don't know how crazy that was: my grandfather had still spoken with a British accent, and my girlfriend had been one of that Brit crowd.

You know what? By 1962 the downstairs pub at the Georgia had been closed for a year, and the arty crowd must have been going somewhere else. I know that the fraternity boys went to the Fraser Arms, and so I still have never been inside that pub. And so now I think I have it right   I was on my way to the Devonshire, even though I had been unjustly arrested in that place two years earlier. Well, we are not going to go over that story.

But I do remember now. There I was, not all that wet except for my hair, in a chair as close to a light bulb as possible, in the pub at the Dev. Conrad or box? Well, my intention had been to sit in a bar with a beer in front of me and read about Marlow. But now here I was, out of the rain, sitting at a table with a small wooden box on it. Having never, I thought, seen the young woman before, and unable to remember what she looked like now, I mean in 1962, I was a little wary. Would my act of untying the twine set off an explosion and render my book unreadable and me blood and guts? I used to imagine myself in international spy escapades whenever I was downtown alone.

I looked around to see whether I could contain the damage if I set off a bomb. The closest drinkers were three tables away. There were two guys in suits at one table, a travelling man with a non-related woman at another, and at a third, a guy in a trench coat. He had his hair combed straight back as if he were an eastern European. When I first looked at him he looked the other way. I was suspicious. His coat was wet.

I took a long sip of my beer. Then I turned the box ninety degrees. I turned it another ninety degrees. I looked up quickly, but the Bulgarian guy was reading some kind of foreign-looking newspaper. The woman with the traveller was looking at me, though. A tiny smile flicked the corners of her mouth. I took a short sip of my beer.

I have always had trouble with knots. When I was a junior high school kid, I had to ask my phys-ed teacher to help me untie the shoelace knots in my sad sneakers. But I carried a Swiss Army knife in the sixties. It would seem, if you have an analytical mind, to make me one of two things, or to tend toward one of those two things — a spy, or a handy woodsy guy like my uncle Gerry.

Uncle Gerry was the manager of the biggest fruit ranch on the east side of Lake Okanagan, a tall thin muscular man with a craggy face. He had been the youngest of his father's eight children and his mother's five. My grandma liked to tell me about his youth, and often called me by his name, or her version of it — Gerald. She liked, for example, to tell me about the sandwiches he made — pork and bean sandwiches, spaghetti sandwiches. He and my dad were each other's favourite siblings. They sat at a card table with a can of tobacco on it. I couldn't imagine them sitting in a pub, though. They didn't even have a beer when they were playing bridge together.

I took out my Swiss Army knife, and noticed that it got

some attention from the eyes in the darkened room. I guess knife blades in beer parlours were something that happened but something people wanted to avoid. I smiled around, indicating that I was not dangerous.

I did pull a knife on a guy once. This happened when I was around fifteen, at Air Cadet camp in Abbotsford. I still have the knife, if you can call it that. I found it one winter after they drained the irrigation ditch that ran south from my home town. It has a kind of homemade look to it. There's a thick pointed solid steel tube we used to call a "toadstabber," and one big rusty blade that would be of no avail if you wanted to carve a pointed stick.

I can't remember the details, but I know that there was this tough guy who was after me for some reason I can't imagine, plus some other guys. I was backed into a corner, and I pulled the toad stabber, but I think it wasn't the toad stabber that made the guy quit. I think it was the desperate wild look in my face. I felt it, that's for sure.

The next night I got my nose broken for the second time, playing catch with a baseball in the advanced dusk of the lower Fraser Valley.

My Swiss Army knife was another matter. It was the exact opposite of homemade looking. I don't remember all the tools there were on it, because I inevitably get it confused with the ones I have had since then, including the one I have now and the one I had to leave at security when I got onto a plane for Ottawa one day last year. Well, the one I have now has a big blade, a little blade, a combination screwdriver–bottle opener–string snapper blade, another kind of screwdriver plus something mysterious with a hook on it, a Phillips screwdriver, a magnifying glass, a pair of scissors, a plastic toothpick, and plastic tweezers. It also has a ring in case I want to attach it by a chain to my belt.

I just now cut my right index finger while opening the small blade.

The guy in the raincoat with the water beading on its surface was not looking at me, not particularly, anyway, when I opened my Swiss Army knife and sawed at the waxy twine tied tight around the box. Ah yes, now I remember, that particular knife had a fish-scaler blade on it.

This is the kind of unwrapper I am. When I have to open a birthday present or Christmas present, which I don't like doing, I am slow and deliberate. I take off the ribbon and roll it into a circle around my fingers, and place it carefully somewhere so that it will not uncoil. Then I meditate for a while. Then I start to take the paper off the present. If there is tape or a gummed seal holding the wrapping together, I peel it carefully, trying not to rip the paper. Part of the reason for this is that my mother always wanted to save the paper for reuse. Not for our family the mountain of ripped holiday paper around the Yule tree. Then I carefully fold the wrapping paper and place it beside the coiled ribbon.

Now it is time to open the cardboard box in which the present is held. Often it will involve white paper wrapped around the slippers or socks or tie or pyjamas or book in the box. I will take out the paper-covered object and put the lid back on the box and place the box beside the wrapping paper and coiled ribbon. Now it is time to meditate again, just for, say, fifteen seconds. Then I remove the white paper, flattening and folding it, even after the slippers have become visible to the naked holiday eye.

So once the waxy twine was severed, I squeezed it into a shape in my hand and walked with it over to the bar and dropped it into the wastebasket on the floor beside the bar. You can leave your beer and cigarettes and book and box on your table, even if you are going to the can, if it is the middle of the afternoon and you are in a downtown bar in a lovely decade when they didn't force loud music into every nook and byway.

The guy in the raincoat watched me all the way to the wastebasket and back, but that could be ordinary, something any single beer drinker might do in a pub such as this. I sat me down and lit up a Sportsman cigarette and did all that stuff that smokers liked doing, closing the ciga-

package, putting the matchbook cover back where it
igs, shifting the ashtray, taking the first drag and put-
the new long cigarette in the ashtray to burn and let up
isp of smoke just as in the ads on the back cover of just
about any popular magazine.

Then I turned the box twice and took hold of the cover.
I thought that it would come off easily, like the covers of
Christmas presents in the movies, but no, it took a bit of
prying. I leaned away from the box as I got the cover finally
off. There was no explosion. There was no bad smell. I put
the box down, and lifted up my cigarette and took a drag
and put the cigarette back in the round glass ashtray. I
looked inside the box.

If this were a made-up story, I might have a little fun
here. I might go to the dictionary I have open on my Qur'an
reader, and pick a noun at random, and make that what was
in the box. For example — well, I will do that right now.
Here's what I will come up with after I have performed this
activity. A frond.

Not very exciting. But maybe it could be worked into something interesting. Fronds are a *little* exotic, aren't they?

But this is not a made-up story. And it was not a frond that
I found inside the wooden box, not a frond that was resting
on the little pillow of stuffed silk on the bottom of the box.
Of course, there is no way you can be sure that I didn't get
what it was out of my dictionary. By the way, the one that
is open on my Qur'an reader is the *Random House Compact Unabridged Dictionary*, the Special Second Edition,
1987. It's pretty big for a compact dictionary, large pages
and 2,230 of them. But believe me, I did not get the chicken
head out of the Random House dictionary.

Not a real chicken head. Not a putrefying barnyard fowl
brain case. Yes, some people will say that chickens don't
have much in the way of brains. I do remember once, when
I was five years old, I saw my dad cutting the head off a
chicken in our back yard, something I was to see more than
once, and more than once I saw the headless chicken try-

ing to go on living. But this once I saw the headless chicken running across the yard, crowing like a scared but entire chicken, and flying up to the low roof over the back yard veranda.

No, no more a real chicken head than the pasha's jewelled scarab is a real insect. This was a conglomeration of jewels and gold in artful imitation or rather copying of a Rhode Island Red's head, and maybe just a bit bigger. I looked at it lying on the cushion in the box, its ruby eye staring at me, or so it seemed. I looked at it for quite a while, trans-as-they-say-fixed, so much so that I was no longer cognizant of anything else going on in the pub. Then I took a drag off my Sportsman, put it back in the ashtray, and picked up the dazzling chicken head.

I turned it round and round. As to the jewels, they were symmetrical in type but not in size, not exactly in size, and this is what made me understand that I was holding something extremely valuable and dangerous. I turned it some more and saw that at the neck end there were two extending bolts of worked gold alloy. With these two bolts it would be impossible to stand the chicken head on a surface such as a table or a shelf. The only practical purpose for them would be connection — with a chicken body, presumably, and if that chicken body were also made of jewels and silver, it would be worth far more than any chicken farm you have ever driven by on the valley highway.

Okay, now I was nervous. I did not grow up in Vancouver, so I still had a sense that it was the exciting and dangerous city down at the Coast. Here now I had a fortune's worth of chicken head, and it had come my way in a manner that I did not understand, and I was in a downtown beer parlour, after all. For all I knew, my Swiss Army knife was the smallest weapon in the immediate area.

So, no, I was not going to have another beer. I gathered up my change, my cigarettes, Joseph Conrad, and the boxed fowl part and headed for the Georgia Street exit. On my way there, I noticed that the guy in the raincoat was nowhere in sight. Had it stopped raining? No, this was Vancouver in January. The pattern of the rain had changed, but it was still raining. I headed toward Granville Street, because that's where my bus stop was. Should I be taking evasive actions to throw off the people tailing me? Should I get on the wrong bus and confuse them? No, because then I would probably find myself alone on the bus with a bad person somewhere way to hell and gone out East Hastings.

I waited, my book and my box sheltered in a movie theatre doorway, until finally the Granville bus came. I'd thought about walking across the bridge and along to our linoleum rooms overlooking False Creek, but I was not easy with bridges. I did think that they were romantic, but whenever I thought of suicide I thought of heading for a bridge. And mysterious disappearances. I know, how many bodies do they find on boats under the bridge? But then, there is the tide, after all, and if used condoms can fetch up on a beach on Passage Island, so can the body of a history student who did not make it across the Granville Street Bridge because of someone with greater skill regarding body mechanics.

A couple of summers earlier I had been with my girlfriend Joan in her father's fourteen-foot inboard boat, learning how to drive for a water skier, and we stopped for a while on the then-unoccupied Passage Island, a little dot of trees and cliffs and one curved beach, off the edge of land most of the way to Horseshoe Bay. The beach was on the city side of the island.

There were used condoms all over the beach. I did not know the word *condom* then, so I must have called them "safes".

"It's amazing," I said, "the number of people who come out here to make out on the beach."

Joan was four years younger than I, but still had ample opportunities to laugh at my naiveté so well fostered by my small town book learning upbringing.

"The tide brings them here," she said. "People flush them down the toilet."

Now there are houses on Passage Island, and the city and environs have a responsible sewage treatment system.

I was not much of a boat driver. I got the gears mixed up and almost killed Joan under one of the cliffs on Passage Island. I don't even think that the term is boat driver. There's got to be a more, I don't know, nautical term.

I had to stand up on the bus, along with quite a few other wet people who were standing up, and right away I started getting the kind of sick feeling you get when the windows are all steamed up and there is too much heat and you don't have enough space and you have to hang onto the bar while hanging onto a book and a box whose lid is no longer tied down. The bus took forever to cross the bridge, and halfway across I decided to wait till Broadway to get off so I could walk on a street with more light and more people than I could count on finding on Seventh Avenue. It would mean walking down the hill to the place that Will Thorne and I laughingly called home, but I liked the odds better. The odds of making it to our linoleum kitchen with a chicken head, without encountering any discouragingly dangerous characters. I mean they would be characters if someone was writing this as a story rather than leaving me to go it alone.

Don't worry. This is not that kind of story. This is a recollection in a series of recollections I seem to be enduring about stuff that happened to me in 1962 or thereabouts.

Why do we say "thereabouts" instead of "thereabout"? Maybe some of you do say "whereabout." According to the aforesaid dictionary, the earliest found use of "whereabout" is in the last half of the thirteenth century, and the earliest found use of "whereabouts" is the first half of the fifteenth century. I am reminded that a little while ago I was wondering why it is that when we are flipping a coin we say "heads" or "tails" even though there is only one coin and hence one of either of those body parts.

When I got off the bus, exiting as I always did from the back door, I was nervous. It was still raining. The lights were all smeary in the wet. I had to cross Granville Street and Broadway, and the wet crowds were pushing the limits at all the traffic lights. I had to hold my book and the box inside my jacket, and avoid being jostled either accidentally or on purpose. I began to wonder whether I would make it to our rickety old house overlooking False Creek's creosote blur. If attacked by a group of violent and persistent strangers, would I throw the box from me or hold tightly, like Hugh McElhenny on his way to first down territory?

This is wholly irrational, I told myself, but I was closer to panic with each step. What could I do? Pitch the box into a dark doorway? What would Conrad's Marlow do? What would Chandler's Marlowe do? What would Christopher Marlowe do? He was reputed to have been a spy. Oh, but he was stabbed to death in a pub. At least I had made it out of the pub. I had Conrad's Marlow under my arm. Why couldn't I have been reading *Victory* instead of *Chance*?

Why couldn't I have been reading Chandler instead of Conrad? At least with Chandler you knew that it was all, finally, in fun, all the murders on rainy streets and so on. Why couldn't I have been writing all this instead of doing it? *The Case of the Chicken's Head*, I thought, and the light indicated that we should walk.

I felt as if I were running around like a chicken with its head cut off, in the rain, with shoes that had ceased to be waterproof before the winter had begun with the storms of November. But I made it across Granville, getting hit in the face once by a wet umbrella and splashed once by a taxi making the corner. After a while I made it across Broadway, and started walking eastward. Broadway is broader than Eighth Avenue or Tenth Avenue, but until 1911 it was officially called Ninth Avenue. In fact, it now turns into Ninth Avenue west of Alma Street, because from there on it is Tenth Avenue that is wider than normal. This is probably because West Point Grey was formerly a separate municipality, separated by forest from Vancouver.

It had been a long time since there had been any forest

anywhere near False Creek. Nowadays False Creek is tour-
ist-and-condo country, but in 1962 it was still dark and oil-
stained, tarpaper and unhealthy fish if any. I turned left and
walked down the steep hill toward the rickety three-story
patched-up house that Will and I had the second floor of.
My heart was actually thumping. My shoes were squish-
ing. I was dying for a cigarette. There was no light on in our
kitchen, where we did all our reading, which meant that
Will was out with his girlfriend, who could cook a lot better than I could.

I climbed the rotting wooden stairs in front, tried to hold
everything under one arm while I searched my pockets for
my key, and searched and searched. I put everything down,
book on top of box, and actually turned out my pockets.
I had a comb and a wallet and a few pennies, the last of
which I threw into the dark street. I would have to go up
the damned ladder again.

Every time I lost my key I had to go up the ladder. It was,
perhaps, a legal fire escape, this ladder nailed to the side of
the old house that waved in a high wind and creaked in a
moderate one. At least this time I was not carrying a case of
beer, and I did not have my arm in a cast as I had had when
I had to climb the ladder in the dark and the rain last September. Now I just had a box with an insecure top, a novel
set in the far southeast, and a hand that was still sore four
months after being broken against a wall that turned out to
be concrete rather than plaster. As you can guess, that, like
a lot of things, is another story.

After reaching the roof at the top of the ladder, and bless-
ing my luck that we did not live on the third floor under a
smaller roof, and pleased that I had not dropped even the
box lid into the murk down below, I made my way across
the curling asphalt shingles and through the kitchen window that we would not have kept locked even if we could.

I toed my soaking shoes off and put them in front of the
heat register, which would make Meredith, the cat that
visited us daily, petulant. I don't know why — it was not

as if the heat very often made its way this high in the
house. Without turning on any light, I put my burden on
the kitchen table, where we kept ashtrays and dictionaries,
and yanked my wet jacket off and hung it on the hook on
the kitchen door, on top of the shop apron Will's peculiar
girlfriend had given to him. I plugged in the kettle, having
ascertained that there was enough instant coffee left for
one cup. Then I sat at the kitchen table and reached into
my shirt pocket for my Sportsmans. Sportsmen? While I
was trying to settle that question, I looked into two eyes
that were shining in the dark because of the uneven light
that made its way into our kitchen from its source over an
automobile dealership up on Broadway.

You probably thought I meant to say "a pair of eyes." In
fact, you probably thought that these two eyes in the dark
of my kitchen belonged to the young woman who gave me
the box, or to the guy in the wet raincoat. You may have
thought that there was a mirror in the kitchen, and that I
mistook my own eyes for a lurker's eyes, the sort of dark
surprise that brings a lone person's heart into his or her
throat.

No such thing. The two eyes belonged to two different
people. One was my roommate Will, and the other was his
girlfriend Yukiko. They were side by side, but on the wrong
side, if you know what I mean. That is, his left eye was to
the right of her right eye. They were clutching each other,
ear against ear, silent as the grave, as they say, though one
wonders whether in that deep quiet darkness you might
be able to hear worms sliding through the dirt and wood.
What a pair of eyes they were. His eye was round, and wide
open, and if the light were on, one could have seen that it
was light green. Hers was dark brown and wide open too,
but not round due to an upper orbito-palpebral sulcus.

My heart was in my throat. I was sitting down at the
kitchen table, or I might have fallen backward against a
wall and hence to the linoleum floor. I heard my name.

"George?"

It was Will's voice. I sat with my elbows on the oilcloth table, breathing like a rescued drowner.

I heard them scrambling, and then Yukiko was sitting on the only other chair, and Will was nearby, somewhere.

"Light," I said.

Will snapped on his cigarette lighter.

"Overhead light," I said, breathing hard.

Then I somehow got my cigarette lit, and when the light came on, I saw that they were only half-dressed. That's the way they had been, in the dark, when they heard someone walking around on the roof outside our kitchen window. They were afraid to turn on the lights, not knowing how many people were out there. It got quiet for a while, and then they heard my footsteps and grunting as I made my way into the place in the gloom.

Normally, I would have eaten the two pieces of sushi that I saw on a plate in front of me.

Next day, when we came home we found the whole place in a hell of a mess. Whoever took the place apart must have made a lot of noise. The little family upstairs, immigrant mother and father and boy child, did not offer us any information, but then we had gone over a month without seeing them once.

There was paper, or rather there were papers, all over the place, on the floor and all the furniture, much of which was on its side. There were new holes in the walls of all three rooms. The kitchen window was left open, and rain had reached halfway across the room. Will's clothes were inside out, torn, and on the floor in the bedroom. My clothes, what there were of them, were likewise disposed in the "living room." The corn flakes box and the shredded wheat box had been emptied onto the kitchen linoleum. Use your imagination — you will see how thoroughly messed up our little dank place was.

As you will have guessed, whoever had made this chaos must have been looking for a jewelled chicken head. But in anticipation of something such as this, I had handed the box to Yukiko to take home with her. She had not wanted to touch the box at first, but Will talked to her in Japanese for a while, and she took it with her. Now even Will and I did not know where it was hidden in the splendid big house where Yukiko made her living as a nanny for a rich doctor and his rich doctor wife.

While we gathered whatever we could salvage from the moist jumble, Will and I discussed the events of the day. I filled him in on the stuff that had happened before I came through the kitchen window in the dark. I did not take the time to discuss Passage Island or the narrative strategies of Joseph Conrad, though Will was interested in Conrad, not only as a storyteller but as a polyglot, for that is what Will was too, though he was still only a young one. Our conversation got round to the danger we felt might pertain to the near future, and we discussed departing our shadowy abode. Next morning we gathered paper and took with us all our written work, all our class essays and notes, and all the short poems we had been knocking off since our freshman year. Will had one that I envied because it started, "Under her taffeta skirt / I searched for the causes of the Punic Wars / While her voice / Promised a dry afternoon for the Island."

Once in a while premonitions seem to carry some weight. When we got off the Broadway bus that afternoon we saw yellow sawhorses blocking our street, and when we got a block down our street we saw that there was just a raggedy pile of charred old boards where our domicile had been. At first I thought: did they burn it down, hoping to find the unmelted chicken head in the black rubble? No, they would not have been allowed to look. No, it would have been destroyed by an unimaginably high temperature. No, this was a demonstration to us that some people did not value human lives as much as they valued some symbolic treasure.

I don't even remember who lived downstairs on the main floor, or whether there was anyone in the basement. We never found out the name of the little family in the two rooms above us. They probably all lost more than we did, because we were just students, and we had taken our essential papers out of the house. But now we did not have a house. Will could not stay with his girlfriend because she was a live-in nanny. I could not stay with my girlfriend because she was staying with her best friend, who was staying with her mother. This best friend would later become a judge, but I never saw her in that capacity.

We did not have many options, as they say, and the worst thing was that whoever burnt our house down would be aware of all the options. This was not a pleasant situation — the semester had two and a half months to go, the big essay-writing season was on us, and we had to figure out how to hide from strangers with low levels of moral and social compunction. To start with, we did what a lot of students did — we lived in Will's car and washed up and so on in the university lavatory. Unfortunately Will's car was a 1956 Morris Minor, a very little car that was for a while more popular among students than any Volkswagen.

The Morris Minor was a tiny fellow, a little bubble with other bubbles for fenders and so on. Its original appellation was the "Mosquito" (pronounced by its British makers "moss-keetow,") probably for its diminutive nature and perhaps for the high pitch of its motor. In 1956, and still in 1962, we and the British still measured things in inches, and the Morris Minor was 148 inches long and 61 inches wide. I was 75 inches long, and Will was 71 inches long. There were four seats in his car. You see our problem.

We did not miss any classes, of course. We were not that kind of boys. And within a week we had a place to live, an old oilstove apartment on the ground floor in lower Kitsilano. For forty dollars a month we got four rooms, two of them actual bedrooms. We went around the neighbourhood looking at handmade signs on poles, and pretty soon we had a bed each and a kitchen table and a big round table for the living room, which became our study room.

We carried chairs from room to room. Will wrote an essay on Tokugawa law, which I would summarize for you, but it really didn't have anything to do with the story. You could say the same for the essay I wrote on Napoleon III.

I was spending a lot of my available research time on various forms of religious ritual involving chickens. The Slavs used to place a round rock with a hole in it in the chicken yard, to protect the chickens from various household gods. Hindus, in some places, tie a chicken by the leg during cremations of their relatives, because a chicken is a magnet for evil spirits. On the other hand, the ancient Greeks considered roosters to be guardians against evil. As for Christians — you will remember that Jesus told Peter that he was expecting him to disavow him three times before the rooster said good morning. The Jews swing a chicken around their heads and slaughter it the day before Yom Kippur. There's a chicken in the Chinese zodiac.

But I could not find any cult that would involve making ornate and bejewelled chicken figurines, life-size or otherwise, much less figurines with detachable heads.

Will and I were awfully busy, what with our assignments and part-time jobs and girlfriends and occasional visit to the Cecil pub. But we did manage to discuss the chicken head, and at greater length, the possible motives for the violence directed our way, or at least my way. In fact, we recorded our discussion on what was then a pretty modern gizmo, my friend Fred's tape recorder, a reel-to-reel item that came with a big Hollywood microphone. I have forgotten most of what was on the tape we made, because it disappeared one day, as things do, as my copy of the original paperback of Jack Kerouac's *Tristessa* did. I hate that. If I had that book that I bought for thirty-five cents in Oroville, Washington a year and a half before this chicken head business, my collection would be complete, more than complete if you count the Kerouac books I have that are in French and Dutch and so on.

I was a little scornful, if I can use that word, of Kerouac

for calling her Tristessa instead of Tristesa. I mean he didn't mention that she was a Basque-Mexican or anything, so why the double ess in her name? Still, I did like reading the novella at the time, and wish that I still had it. I have it in German, but still. I mean even if I spent a lot of money and bought a copy of the original Avon mass-market paperback. If the person who stole it from me is reading this, well, I'm glad you had the interest to read this.

But for some reason, maybe an assignment, maybe a dumb hope of selling a story to a newspaper, we transcribed some of the tape. The few pages of double-spaced typewritten dialogue were in a folder along with the transcription of a taped interview we did — Will and I — of a radio host asking questions of a guy who got famous for tracking down and consuming cat puke. That one will never get into a story.

"... to know is, what's with the two pointy things coming down from the chicken's head?"

"Cock."

"No, thanks."

"No, I mean I think it might be what you Protestants call a rooster."

"You're a Protestant, too."

"Okay. Let's not let this get frayed into needless asides and diversions. You were wondering about the spike-like things that would prevent you from placing the cock's head vertical on a smooth surface such as this kitchen table."

"Screw."

"Haven't got time."

"No, I mean they're more screw-like things than spike-like things."

"But as there are two of them, one could not screw the head into anything."

"Okay, no screwing around. But they look as if one is supposed to push them into something, sort of like pushing a plug into a wall socket."

"You think that the jewel-encrusted head is a night light?"

"On the contrary — it is a source of darkness, in the business of mystery-solving."

"Obviously the most likely case is the case of the jewel-encrusted, headless, chicken body."

"Unless the body is without jewels. Maybe it is just something to hold the obviously priceless head. Kind of a fowl jewel box."

"Hmm. Of course, we might be looking at this from the wrong angle altogether. Maybe the object that has two wormholes corresponding to the points on the head part is a bomb. It would not matter whether it is in the shape of a Rhode Island Red or simply a cube. Once the head is inserted into the receptacle, the mechanism is begun, and the inserter has to hightail it for safety."

"Ah, if you weren't my friend and acolyte, I would proclaim you a genius. But now we have to leap even beyond that certainty into another world of puzzlement. That is: why did someone force the precious and dangerous object on me, and why are they trying to homicide me to get it back?"

"Why do I get the rumble seat ride?"

"I beg your pardon?"

"Learned reference. Meant for the most astute of readers."

"There are no readers. This is a conversation in our new temporary home, or more specifically, in a cold kitchen in Kitsilano."

"Damn. That's poetry."

"I'll poetry you, young man."

"And that's ... "

We had a lot of conversations of a similar structure in those days of the early sixties, just before the sixties happened, but the sixties were an ongoing media event, and the sixties started around 1957, if you are talking prose fiction, or around June 22nd, 1945, if you are talking music. As a matter of fact, I came more and more to think that my life was characterized by the structure that characterized those conversations, and I don't know which influenced which. But it was around 1962 that I vowed to tell stories with a straight-ahead order, the way that Hemingway did, to save some clarity out of the disorder around us.

Will has always been nuts about Hemingway, but I am not going to get into that here. After all, Hemingway wrote *Across the River and Into the Trees*, but here we are not interested in why the officer crossed the river, if you see what I am saying.

Okay, so we were evidently yucking it up in those days (as we do today, forty-five years later). But we were living in fear. You could say that the fear of being blown to smithereens, or jonesereens, as Will called them, would be a sure way of getting our attention away from the fear of academic failure. I know that when I turned out my reading light at 3:00 every night or morning or whatever you prefer to call it, I scanned the darkness I had made for sudden death. Normally you would not call our new neighbourhood dangerous, but we felt that we had good reason to listen hard for sounds outside our bedroom windows. Will's window was on the back alley, and mine was on sloping Yew Street. There were enough sounds to bring this kind of conversation over the morning instant coffee:

"I think we ought to give them the chicken head and live a long fruitful life as wage earners."

"Listen, Will, the jewels on that head will be our retirement fund in about forty years. Let them be satisfied with whatever that poultry's body might contain."

Then we relaxed ever so slightly.

Until one morning we opened the door to the hallway and found that we had to step over or pick up the headless body of a Chantecler.

There are so many things named after that particular breed of yard bird. I think that there is a cigarette rolling

paper with that name and a picture of a proud fowl on the
package. There's a fancy hotel in the Laurentian mountains
back of Montreal. There's a famous Italian jeweler —

Wait a minute. Was that a clue? I certainly did not think
of it at the time, probably because I had never heard of any
famous Italian jeweler at the time. But in 1962 the jet set
was all the rage, and so was the Isle of Capri. Chantecler the
jet set's jeweler was romanced by celebrities at his palace
on the Isle of Capri. I imagined standing beneath the shade
of an old walnut tree. Are you with me?

Okay, that headless poultry on the floor outside our door
made us nervous. Speaking for myself, I can say that I was
alert all day, sitting close to the door in classrooms, darting
looks in every direction when I was outdoors, peeking carefully inside my tuna fish sandwich.

But the day transpired and so did the next, and soon I
managed to walk without my hand on the imaginary hand-
gun in my pocket. I slowed down my research of chickens
and jewels and returned full force (well ...) to my school
work. I wanted to be a Master of Arts more than I wanted
to be an orchard worker. Will was gearing up to be a French
teacher. I told him that he was trying to justify all the
smutty novels he kept acquiring at the French bookstore
downtown.

Then Will's girlfriend disappeared. She left a very short
note for her employers but said nothing of where she was
going or when she might be expected back. She left no word
for Will at all.

"This is not like Yukiko," he said.

"Then who *is* it like?" I asked.

But I don't think that either of us was looking for a com-
parison. Will was, after his five words, one of them a proper
noun, speechless. A lot of bad things had happened in his
life, so I knew that either (a) he would manage to continue,
or (b) the accumulated nastiness of life would cause him to
go over the edge. I hated to think of which edge, so I went
with (a). My girlfriend was on a diving trip with another

young man, so I was more blasé than Will was. In fact, I
didn't know whether he was, as I was, giving thought to the
fact that without Yukiko we had no clue as to where the
jeweled chicken head was. If Will and I had been two other
guys, in fiction or in our rainy lives, we might have had a
tale of betrayal here — sidekick and gal take off with treasure, leave would-be novelist in bitter poverty.

I'd like to tell you that I know where the chicken head
went. Yukiko and I met a year later on the coast of Guate-
mala and lived for several years by prising an amethyst or
ruby off the gold once in a while. We adored one another's
flesh and created sunny babies who grew up speaking
Spanish.

Nope. Will did get one letter from her in 1963, just about
the time that he was polishing his thesis on the role of
nineteenth-century French fiction in the British Columbia
classroom. She told him that she had a very high regard for
him, and that he should forget all about her and everything
that had happened. She hoped that he would have a very
satisfying career as a teacher. She did not have a message
for me. But as you see, there was one.

So I have lived in uncertainty all the rest of my life. I don't
look over my shoulder as often as I used to, but I do it some.
If that jewelled head was or is really old, like hundreds of
years old, like those rifles and saddles in the Topkapi Palace, then the hunt for it would not be a short-term thing.
What do a few decades of my life mean compared to something like a dynastic or holy quest for lost family or proph-
et's treasure? You see what I mean? But if the agents that
burn down houses also kidnap and murder young Asiatic
women, or make deals with them, then there is no reason
that the terrorists would be interested in me anymore.

So I say: if that is the case, why couldn't they at least *tell*
me?

☐ Belief

I believe he had seen us out of the window coming off to dine in the dinghy of a fourteen-ton yawl belonging to Marlow my host and skipper.

You probably don't know who or what I am referring to in my use of the pronoun "I", and I imagine that that will be true, also, regarding the times I use it in this sentence about that first one. Or should I say "I" imagine, but then would that not be "I" imagines? You see the sort of problem a person has in trying to tell a story or relate an anecdote or make a confession in the first person. Whose idea was it to call "I" the first person in the first place? Surely there are people whose mindset or religion, or just plain good manners, would see nothing untoward in calling you the first person, or him the first person.

It could be a matter of adapting to the situation. If I were to say, "I saw him smile as he received the award from the hands of the governor-general," you might say that I was being only sensible if I were to call the award-winner the first person in this circumstance. Or, say, Marlow, when I saw his smile when he knew himself to be the first skipper under the harbour bridge at the end of the Celebes run.

In any case, we have to start somewhere, so we will have to come to an agreement here that this "I" is I, either this person sitting here typing these words, or the one we agree to listen to while he or she tells this tale of the odd young man whose name you have not yet heard.

It is all a matter of chance. That is why I may not have chosen the best possible verb when I chose "believe." I say this even though I know that the end of my story will come when Marlow uses the word. He will say, "Hang it all, for all my belief in Chance I am not exactly a pagan . . . " Ever since I heard him utter that sentence, if that is the whole of the sentence, I have wondered how ironic he was being. Of course, when it comes to the interplay of belief and chance, how could one not be ironic? It is just, I think, a matter of degree.

"It is my belief," he once told me just after we had experienced a terrific storm off Malacca, "that we have no justification in holding to any belief system, as much as we might desire that it may work."

I told him that I had prayed while his ship lay nearly on its side atop a thirty-foot wave.

"Do you *believe*," he asked me, "that your prayer brought us through?" He looked a little like a Buddha in the evening light. "I was told not long ago a tale of four men set adrift in a lifeboat off the coast of Florida. When their boat ran in on the reef, it was battered to pieces, and three of the four castaways died. The best among them drowned, and a brute with murderous intent was left to live. I do not know how many of these four prayed during their ordeal, nor what they prayed for."

I think that I have heard a thousand stories from Marlow. And I am pretty sure that he could have strung this one out so that it lasted several hours, or, let us say, a hundred pages or more. I know that it is a cliché to have sea captains reciting tales, but there you are — I oftentimes think that Marlow was created for the job.

In any case, I am willing to replace the word "believe" with "think," though there are problems there, too. For example, are we really justified in calling what I was doing

thought? Let's let it go, and say something about this "he,"
I believe — think — I saw. I don't know why I merely used
the pronoun rather than the man's name, or why I did not
begin by telling you something about him. He is, as you
can easily infer from my sentence, going to be an important
personage in my account, just as he or his pronoun seems
to be the centre of the topic sentence you have been fortun-
ate enough to see or hear.

I believe — think — that starting a story or even a novel
in this fashion, a kind of *in media res*, is fairly common in
recent literature. Certainly, around the time of the beginning of the First World War it would have been done by
the fiction writers who situated themselves forward of the
general popular writing. When you see or hear me utter
the pronoun "he" you expect that to be narrowed down in
due time. I think, *think*, that there have been writers who
fancy themselves as experimental, who give no more personal information than the pronoun all the way through
the piece or book in question.

Does that sort of thing happen in real life, you ask. Certainly not. Not a chance. It is a sure sign of design, of purpose. Or maybe not: maybe the writer who refuses anything more than the gendered pronoun is trying to imitate
what your senses do in any passage through a day. That is,
you notice, by sight and sound, a person, even a person you
know, but you do not consciously say his name, aloud or
inwardly. You leave it at "he."

Enough of that. I am not a literary theorist, you will be
glad to learn, and we are not here for theory. We are here
for clarity. That is why I am taking a little time to expound
upon my topic sentence.

So we have an "I" and a "he." That is not bad when it
comes to populating a tale. And you already know that
there is a third, my host and skipper. Chances are, you have
run into him before, especially if you frequent waterfront
towns such as this one.

I am sure that we do not have to long consider the word

"had", as it only serves to signify a tense, in this case the pluperfect. Doing that, it clarifies, or complicates, the time frame of the events to be reported. Well, some of that is inevitable. If I am going to recount these events in the normal past tense, I am going to have to use the pluperfect. If I were talking to you on the way to the ship, I might use the preterit, or possibly the imperfect. But starting with the pluperfect, I am preparing you for the phenomenon you will encounter within a few pages — quotation marks within quotation marks.

So: I "believe" he had seen us. That "us" joins the other pronouns we have been discussing, or which, actually, I have been writing and you have been reading. The difference here is that you will not yet know the number of people thus referred to, if you do not mind my hanging a preposition there. And why would you if you do not mind the ambiguities in my sentence that would suggest, among other things, eating in a dinghy.

In my next sentence, which we will not see for a while, you will learn that the "we" there employed will designate at least three people, and in fact in what should have been a very short while, you will find that that will be the number. Three. The boy, Marlow, and I, or in the case of the first sentence, me.

I do not think that we have to contemplate or argue the single words that follow. I *think* that we can consider "out of the window" all at one time. Normally I would say "out the window," but we have a distinctly British, if tropical, setting here, or instance, let us say. And I believe, or sense, that the Brits double up on (hee hee) their prepositions. So it is out of the window.

You will learn in time that the window in question is the window of a riverside inn, where Powell, for that will be discovered to be his name, was dining at a long table as white and inhospitable as a bank of snow. I think that was the simile that came immediately to my mind, at least.

But you see what engineering I am endeavouring to pull

off here, as I lay about me with your perceptions, or the imaginary ones I hope to invoke. There is the question of the pluperfect, of course, but here you are behind some window where someone is catching sight of your narrator and his companion, all this a matter of belief. It is even more complicated than that, but you see what direction I am sending your observation in. The optic heart must venture, as someone more recently said.

I had reason sometime later, I thought, to wonder whether he had "chanced" to see us from his vantage point. Youth was my lot in those days, and my aim as well as my duty was to listen to these two old seamen tell their tales.

It is true that there was nothing unusual in his choice of dining rooms. The inn was the only place along the river in which one might get decent European fare unless one were to climb a distance that would be equal to a dozen blocks in a British or German city. And there was likely no contrivance in his choice of a seat facing the window and its view of the landing stage. I would not call it chance, but I would call it normal. And his being there just when we were on our way? It could have been chance.

Marlow was always going on about chance with a capital *C*. It was like the religion of no religion for him. More than once he would make pronouncements about it in my hearing.

"But from that same provision of understanding," the atheist would say, "there springs in us compassion, charity, indignation, the sense of solidarity; and in minds of any largeness an inclination to that indulgence which is next door to affection."

This was the way in which Marlow would construct a conversational sentence, so there should be no animus against mine.

Once on a night-time pier, I heard a dying man offer Marlow's sentiment in more direct and far less encourageable language. "A man alone," this unfortunate said, "hasn't got a f—— chance."

It has always struck me that this kind of usage of that final word is almost an opposite to the other.

In any case, this so-far unmet old seaman observed our coming off, and probably from that moment arranged things so that our meeting and spinning of yarns was anything but accidental. Certainly we had no idea that we were being watched, and no idea that we would spend that evening and many others with the watcher. He was a man who could not adjust to his retirement on shore, and who often looked for someone such as Marlow, whom he recognized if he did not know him.

He it was who once remarked that Nietzsche said that there are two kinds of people — those who want to know and those who want to believe. I reckon that people in the latter group are not much interested in anything I have to write.

But what will you know? Do you know more now than our watcher knows by this point in the story? Can a character know more than his watcher, or rather reader? Certainly he seems to, as for example, he likely knows his name and his version, anyway, of his life story, before you open the book. But can he be said to exist at all before you open and read?

That is not exactly the sort of situation that he and Marlow conversed about that evening and those to come, but there is a similarity in form, or let us say in structure. He was watching us, as you are watching him, and certainly Marlow has seen this sort of thing so often, he the beginner of long tales. Romance never knew a better partner.

But as I have said, we came off not to spin yarns but to dine. I honestly do not know whether Marlow the Buddha ever tasted any of the food that passed between his lips. Observing him at the board, one might surmise that he was there for the carrying out of a secular ritual. He might sever a morsel from a chop while listening to an opinion offered by the man with the red-tinted face and cap of curly iron-grey hair. But then his utensils would be the shining ends for gestures he might make to indicate the breadth of the Indian Ocean or the lawlessness on some of its islands.

In other words, to dine, for Marlow, is to meet the necessity of the body's sustenance. Necessity, you will point out, is the opposite of chance. I might counter that the opposite of some instance of chance is another instance of chance. Let us say that for Marlow, the need to dine is the opportunity to dramatize folly and honour.

Then there is the storyteller's necessity. Since the dawn of writing, at least, the meal has been the setting for accounts sacred and profane, entertaining and philosophical. We know Socrates and Alcibiades by the reasoning and wit they exhibited during their symposium. We listened while Jesus foretold his story at the Last Supper. But we also know that we have told and heard wonderful baloney around a campfire, and fancy that right after fire was domesticated, hairy men stared into it and commenced lying to one another about their exploits with spears and such.

"Dine in the dinghy" is a misleading and quite comical phrase, and one that I might change if I could, but it is as if the sentence had been passed down to me in its present form and I incapable of changing a word. I may asseverate but never slice. I might wiggle some, but must remain within the tides.

As chance might have it, "dinghy" follows three words after "dine" on page 157 of Partridge, just as it does in my sentence. Does that not sound like design? Remember Marlow, who said, "I am not afraid of going to church with a friend." If Marlow found a watch on a supposedly deserted island, he would reason that a wayfarer had been there before him, not that a deity had dropped the timepiece to prove a point.

What does Partridge tell us of a dinghy, seeing that we are there anyway? "Bengalese *dingi*, dim of *dinga*, a boat; ? from Skt *dru*, wood (cf the Gr *drus* s *dru-*, the oak).

What an interesting page. Did you know that our word "dip" is related to the OS *dopian* (with a little circle over

the *o*), to baptize. But there you go; the last thing we want
to do here is to stray from the story. I mean, every page
in Partridge is interesting. A fire engine coming out of its
garage.

A diminutive boat coming out of its element onto shore
at dinnertime. Two of us stepped out. The lad would return
for us when he received Marlow's signal in the dark, and if
precedent be a guide, the youth might be able to get some
sleep before that event. He pushed off without our help,
and we walked up to the boards that would lead to the res-
taurant. We arrived there just as the floating wood made it
home to the fourteen-ton yawl.

Fourteen tons is a pretty fair weight for a yawl, most of
the ones I have seen being perhaps three tons. Marlow never
used the term — he always referred to her as a "dandy."
Marlow has been skipper of a lot of vessels in his day and
ours. I believe or imagine, let us say, that he favoured a
yawl because with its mizzen-mast abaft the rudder, he
could trim delicately. This would mean that he could keep
a small crew. I have often seen one of the smaller yawls
crewed by a single man. At the moment our crew numbered
eight, largely because stevedores can be hard to find in the
unofficial, let us say, harbours to which we pay visit.

One foggy day in 1905, two fourteen-ton yawls carrying
nothing but ballast collided and sank off Donegal Town.
This despite the advantages of the mizzens. One of them
was named *Maid of Erin*. The other bore the interesting
cognomen *Victory*. You could, as an American friend often
tells me, look it up.

Chance threw them, Marlow told me one damp night, in
one another's way.

How long this particular yawl had belonged to Marlow,
I never sought to learn from him. One got the impression
that the craft had a past unknown to him, and an even
stronger sense that he had been the owner or at least skipper of a long list of vessels of many sorts. I more than once
heard that he had negotiated the Congo River at the helm

of some sort of paddlewheeler, and that there had at least on one occasion been only a shadow line between his occupation and that of a brigand, this somewhere that British institutions had never rubbed smooth.

But in another sense it seemed as though the rig and its owner were almost indistinguishable. They were both weathered and brown and of an undeniable age. They both, one fancied, had unfinishable tales to tell. They both creaked when they moved.

I was then amazed and have since been astonished that Marlow is not the most famous man in the Empire. If all his stories have secure attachment to the real events of his watchful life, he is Homer for our time. And I have heard sufficient allusions to both his history and his historifying to believe (or assent) that the untapped narratives might be more resourceful than those I had (to return to the pluperfect) been vouchsafed.

Marlow was, in the rivermouths of the eastern hemisphere, ubiquitous — yet he was mysterious. I have heard people compare him with a god and an idol, with a statue of the Buddha and a wrinkled bird of the jungle canopy. I have pulled my watch from my vest and been astounded to see that four hours had slipped by while he smoked his pipe and told us about conflict in the heart of a man encountered belowdecks.

In his stories he was always marling such things.

I sometimes thought that Marlow had been invented by some overarching intelligence to frequent the waters of the colonized world and bring doubt into the minds of anyone, east or west, about the intentions of the European colonizers. All of Europe, he once told me, went into the making of a monster named Kurtz. In our nightly discussions with Mr. Powell, this question always lay in the background: How was it that Powell had retired to a land so far from his bringing up, and how was it that Marlow, easily his equal in years, seemed bound for an eternity on the water?

Perhaps a coming together of two such differing fates was

necessary to the story — for it was not long until we would discover that Marlow knew the young Powell, and understood a key factor in his life — that young Powell had by mere chance received his first posting as second-in-command, and that by that accident was the whole course of his life directed — his and those of numerous others. Well, you will see. You will sit at Marlow's table or on his deck. You will decide whether we are dealing with design as introduced to us by the European Greeks, or chance, a word, Partridge reminds us, that like many others descends from the Skt çad-, to fall.

Not to jump, eh?

By "my host" I mean principally my host at the dinner to come, or as we will see it or now do see it, depending on whether we are inside or outside the narrative, the dinner that ensued. Well, enough of that mumble — you have by now seen my point regarding that. Marlow had noticed that I was careful with my ready money once ashore. He did not know my reason, and certainly there is no need for you to know it. Suffice it to say that any money I came upon was required in a coastal town on the other side of the sphere upon whose surface we sail.

Marlow sensed my situation, but was too much an officer of the old school to pry. He told me that in buying my supper he was ensuring himself an audience for his hoary narratives. Then he busied himself with his pipe. He was an actor with sufficient skill and experience to play himself. I directed mental plaudits his way and looked forward to filling my stomach more than usual.

As Marlow liked the term "dandy" in reference to his vessel, I like the term "skipper" in reference to its master. I know that he did. He was uneasy with the appellation "captain" because it has the word for head in it. Perhaps that displeased him because he was opposed to the hierarchy or governance proposed, seeing himself as he was in his youth, a soul setting to sea because the sea and its unknown resembles hope, resembles in its promise of chance a great possibility that no god or empire would extend to a fellow. Certainly a captain is *enmeshed*, both in his history and in rank.

Perhaps he did not like the word "head" because he had learned over a long career among dark trees and mirror-like water, that the head as the imperium of the living organism is a conceit that loses its usefulness upon the part of any journey that leaves Europe astern.

Besides, he did not want to dress up as a captain.

"Sir," I once gathered the nerve to say, "there is a recollection of last night's curry upon the back of your jacket sleeve."

"Where it will stay," he replied, never taking his eye off the azimuth, "until I require sustenance enough to search it out."

So "skipper," a word that is simply connected to the word "ship." Important here is my reference to him as *my* skipper. That is the relationship and debt that I want to keep visible when I get to my next sentence, for there it is that you will see us working together, not head and arms but arms bent to our mutual task.

Or if I abandon you to carry on the story by yourself, I hope that you do it with the "dignified loneliness" that I would have attributed to old Mr. Powell in that second sentence. It was going to be a long one, and the story too. I hope that you will include me among your listeners when you happen upon this.

☐ Watson's Rainbow

You have read all kinds of stories about some ball player or maybe a whole team that is mired in a slump so bad that it has to be funny, but then maybe it is too long to be funny, and maybe this player consults a voodoo man or makes a deal with the devil or something, and if there is a happy ending it gets really funny again. But do you know the story of Bunny Watson, left-handed fireball pitcher with the Vancouver Mounties in the AAA Pacific Coast League in 1962?

I have to remind you, maybe, that the 1962 season in Vancouver was kind of funny for other reasons. In the second game of a doubleheader on July 18, manager Jack McKeon, who would win a world series with the Florida Marlins forty-one years later, stuck a radio receiver into a pocket under the jersey of his ace pitcher George Bamberger. It wasn't that Jack was going to tell Bamberger what to do. Bamberger was the most famous pitcher in the Pacific Coast League, and knew more than anyone in the world what to throw at the starting lineup of the Tacoma Giants. Jack just wanted to see whether he could get away with it.

You could look it up. The radio kit was approved by the Canadian government, and had the call letters XM11495.

The Mounties won the game 8–4, if you are interested in that stuff, but this isn't about Jack and Bamby. It's about the fellow that started the Mounties season as their number four starter — and that was back when teams had a four-man rotation, and the starters didn't come tiptoeing off the mound after a hundred pitches.

The fellow in question was Bunny Watson, and if you are an old fart like me, who hung around Capilano Stadium in 1962, you remember a skinny guy with huge arms, about six foot three, with shoes so big that when he went into his high kick his right foot put a little shadow in the area around home plate.

Okay, if I start to exaggerate, that means I am turning into one of those old-fashioned baseball writers, call themselves "scribes." You are free to complain any time I start exaggerating for comic effect. But Bunny did have enormous feet.

Bunny had been a bonus baby in 1955, getting $100,000 from the New York Yankees, and sitting on their bench for two years. That was the rule: any high school or college kid who got a big signing bonus had to stay with the major-league team for two seasons. It worked for Sandy Koufax and the Dodgers: he was a mature fireballer at age twelve, for goodness' sake. The Twins did okay with Harmon Killebrew, who started on his Hall of Fame career from day one. But most bonus babies sat on the bench, getting up once in a while to pinch-run, or throw a late inning in a 12–0 game.

Bunny Watson got two stolen bases in four attempts in 1955. In 1956 he got into eleven games, throwing fifteen and a third innings, and going 0–1 with a 6.45 ERA. In those days the legal maximum for a signing bonus was $100,000, but rumour had it that Bunny got pretty near twice that from the Yankees, one of the few teams that could afford it. You can figure out how much he was getting paid per inning. Don't forget to factor in his rookie salary, $5,000.

In 1957, as soon as he was legally able to, Casey Stengel sent Bunny down to AA ball, where he could get some innings in. He stayed there for the first half of 1958 and then was promoted to AAA; but in 1959, he joined the legion of unknown players sent by the Yankees to Kansas City in trade for future stars. Bunny went down and played for the Little Rock Travelers, a team that was not known for pummelling the baseball, and then he kept coming up to the Athletics, if that is not a contradiction in terms, then going back down, until the Washington Senators moved to Minneapolis and scooped him up by way of waivers. By that time a lot of the young people he was playing ball with were entirely ignorant of his history as a bonus baby.

In 1961 the Berlin Wall went up, and Bunny Watson spent the season with the brand new Minnesota Twins. They even let him pitch over two hundred innings. He felt as if he were back in Little Rock, as the Minnesota hitters let him down, and he put in a record of 4–18. The Twins told him that he was likely to be in the Pacific Coast League for the start of the 1962 season. It had been nearly seven years since he'd got his bonus. After seven years most of the bonus babies were pretty well broke, but Bunny's dad was one of those new-fangled investment consultants with an office in Boise. By December of 1961 Bunny Watson had about a quarter of a million dollars in real estate and a chequing account. But he also had an ERA of 5.25.

Every off-season till then, he had spent his mornings running alongside rural roads, and his afternoons chopping wood and doing push-ups. In December 1961 he said to hell with it, he was going to try something else. He thought about going to Berlin to visit the home of his mother's grandparents, but the Twins said no deal — he might get stuck on the wrong side of the Wall. So he went to Ireland. He didn't have any great grandparents in Ireland. He just liked the idea of shamrocks and shillelaghs, all the stuff the popular press and advertising people in New York and Boston liked so much. Heck, he had been born four days after St. Patrick's Day. Close enough. He packed all his green clothes and hopped a DC–8 for Shannon.

For a few days he looked around at the Georgian buildings, and sat down in genuine Irish pubs with genuine Irish
whisky, but this was not the Ireland he had always dreamed
of. The Ireland he had always dreamed of featured donkey
carts and stone fences and peat hillsides. So he got himself a
tweed backpack and a stout stick, and began his rural walking, along lanes and on eskers overlooking brownish water
pushing against lichen-covered rocks, all that sort of thing.
He carried with him two volumes of Sean O'Casey's plays
because he had been lucky enough to catch a production of
The Plough and the Stars in Chicago one night after a day
game against the White Sox. When he bought the books in
Dublin the young man who took his money had curled his
lip when he pronounced the playwright's name.

A good reason for getting out of Dublin was the chocolate bars. He had never seen such a city for chocolate bars.
Everywhere you went you saw people eating chocolate bars.
On the street, on the buses. Poor people. Well-to-do-people.
Business people. Even in the pubs you saw people standing with a Guinness in one hand and a chocolate bar in
the other. Bunny had to get away from all this chocolate-
munching. He stuck a dozen apples into his tweed backpack and headed for the treeless country.

One foggy morning he was walking on the Esker Riada
alongside the Shannon River near the ruins of Clonmac-
noise. On foggy mornings in the centre of Ireland it is usually quiet, save for the odd overflight of Irish Air Corps CM
170s often invisible in the mist. But this quiet morning all
Bunny heard was the crunch his front teeth made into an
Irish apple. Well, that is all he heard until the angry little
voice.

He followed this novelty until he came upon a sight that
made him want to (a) laugh out loud or (b) turn tail and ske-
daddle. No wonder he could not make out what the angry
little voice was saying. All Bunny could see was the bottom
half of a very little person sticking up into the air, legs gyr-
ating, little seat humping back and forth. The creature's top

half was poked into a hole in the ground, and the sound that came out was muffled by the tight squeeze, thin in pitch due to the small size of the person it emerged from, and in a language other than English. Irish, Bunny figured.

He put his tweed backpack down on the boggy ground, seized the little ankles, and yanked the expostulating wee fellow out of the hole.

"*Buíochas le Dia!*"

The critter was bashing himself around the head and neck, trying to get wet dirt off.

"Hold it," said Bunny. "Do you speak English?"

The little guy started to move off, but Bunny grabbed him, and now he did not let him go. The little guy was about the size of a large Chihuahua dog.

"Shore 'n' beggorah," said the little guy.

"English," said Bunny.

"Damn!"

"That's better," said Bunny.

"I mean it. Damn!"

"Damn what? I got you out of the hole. What were you doing in the hole, anyway?"

"I am not obliged to tell you that. You were just lucky."

"*I* was lucky? *I* was lucky! Hah, you are one lucky leprechaun, buddy."

"We don't use that word. It's demeaning. How would you like to be called Lefty?"

"I *am* called Lefty."

"Well, we are called the Little People."

Bunny hung on tight to the Little Person, knowing that he would scamper away if he could. The little person had a little white beard and a bit of a tummy, but he looked fit. He cursed, it seemed to Bunny, in his own language, and then said damn a few more times in English.

"Why do you claim that *I'm* the lucky one?" asked Bunny Watson, who had not used that word to describe himself over five baseball seasons.

"Ah, you are a foreigner. I can tell by your uncouth

speech," said the little person. "Nevertheless, I am bound by a law older than that crumbled church over there, to tell you the rules. If you manage, through some incredible stroke of good fortune, to nab one of us and hold on, we must reward you."

"I like it," said Bunny. "But don't call it luck. It's skill. Years of conditioning and sacrifice have paid off."

"Oh, don't give me that sacrifice business. You sound like an Olympic athlete."

Bunny thought of stuffing this cranky little bugger back into the hole, but he was curious, and he was a fan of all things Irish.

"Okay, what about the reward? It had better have nothing to do with chocolate bars."

"Traditionally, you will be wanting me to show you where my pot of gold is hidden. I'll be the laughing stock of the Little World from Athlone to Kildare."

Bunny snorted.

"I don't need your gold. I'm a bonus baby."

"*Go n-ithe an cat thú is go n-ithe an diabhal an cat!*"

Bunny squeezed.

"English!"

"All right. No gold. What do you want instead of gold, my fine young foreign moron?"

"Well, last summer I went 4–18."

The 1962 Vancouver Mounties were not a powerhouse, but they played one of the most interesting seasons in the history of the Pacific Coast League, what with George Bamberger's shirt pocket radio and the UFO. Maybe we will get to the UFO later.

Bamberger was the long-time ace for the Mounties, of course. He was one of those guys, like Lefty O'Doul, who preferred to stay in the nice climate of the Pacific Coast League, so when the Vancouver franchise was passed from Baltimore to Milwaukee to Minnesota, and all the other players moved on, Bamby just stayed in town. On opening day, Bamberger used his 80-mph fastball and his smarts to down Tacoma. Then the Mounties lost two games, and the stage was set for their number four starter, Bunny Watson.

It was not an auspicious start. The sky was blue, and there was a light breeze, but it was not warm enough to make you sweat in your sweatshirt. Bunny had his fastball working, and his slider was on the verge of sliding. In the seventh inning he was behind 6–5, and working slowly, or as they say around ballparks, slow. He saw a right-handed person whose name he had not yet learned getting loose in the Mounties bullpen down by the left field foul pole. That was just enough to get him through the seventh with no further damage, but his arm felt as if someone had injected it with mercury. If Jack McKeon asked him whether he had another inning in him, he would be honest with him.

He was due up third in the bottom of the seventh, so chances were that Jack was going to yank him, anyway. As fate would have it, he was fidgeting around in the on-deck circle when Julio Becquer banged a one-out double into the gap. Now, Bunny was a .083 lifetime hitter in the minors, so he was already walking back to the dugout when Julio performed an unnecessary stand-up slide at second. The guy who hit for him, Chuck Weatherspoon, nearly lost every item of clothing he was wearing when he swung at the first pitch, lofting the horsehide (as it still was in those days) high into the spring air. The centre fielder knew just where it was going to come down, as centre fielders, though not holding degrees in physics, seem to do, and headed for the fence.

He ignored the warning of the warning track, and leapt high against the painted plywood, his raised glove touching it just a foot below the spot where the baseball bounced off. The entire list of Pacific Coast League historians and fans regrets that there were no television cameras in Capilano Stadium, no slow-motion replay, no recording whatsoever. The centre fielder was going at a terrific rate, and when the baseball came down off the fence, it hit him on the top of his head, apparently, and his momentum propelled it right over the wall for a two-run homer.

The unnamed right-hander pitched two lovely innings of relief, and Bunny Watson, at 1–0, had his first winning record in three years.

The Vancouver papers had a good time describing the wonder, and the morning paper even printed a photo of the outfield, with a dotted line illustrating the course of the mighty blow. This was in 1962, remember, before the Vancouver papers decided that hockey and football should fill the sports pages during baseball season.

Less than a week later Bunny was working the mound in Spokane, where the air was already Inland Empire hot and often filled with dust going around in circles. He was not overpowering the Indians, but after seven innings his arm felt only a little bit heavy, and his fastball was still veering off in some unpredictable direction ten feet in front of the plate. When your slider is not sliding all that much, it is nice to have some action on your heater. In any case, the Mounties and the Indians were deadlocked at five when Bunny came to bat in the seventh, a man on second and one out. He was hitting .000 on the season, with no other offensive stats.

But somehow, somehow, he got the fat part of the bat on a big fat fastball that didn't fast. This luck eventuated in a ground ball that slowed down dramatically in front of the second baseman. This fellow headed in practiced fashion toward the spheroid, but managed only two steps before falling on his face. The shortstop then scampered after the ball, which had almost come to a stop, but he too fell on his face.

The runner who had been on second was rounding the bag at third, when the pitcher fell on his face after one step toward the ball. Bunny was safe at first, dancing around, waving his arms, threatening to stretch his single into a double. He could have made it too; no one had picked up the ball.

The Indians mounted, as they say, a threat in the bottom of the ninth, but the young right-hander came in with one out and two on, and struck out the last two volunteers at the plate. Bunny was 2–0 on the season, ahead of George Bamberger in the win column.

You'd have to say that luck had a lot to do with it. Bunny was not exactly mowing them down, and his ERA was nothing to write home — or Minneapolis — about. Something similar was happening in his love life. She was not a Baseball Annie — in fact, until meeting Bunny Watson, she had never been to a professional ball game. Corny as it was, they met in front of the monkey cage at Stanley Park. The monkeys had a cage in front, and an island out back, rocks and trees and monkey stuff surrounded by a little lake of salt water in which the seals swam. When she walked from the glass front of the cage around to the seal part, he just plain followed her. Her name was Linda, of course, this being 1962, and she did not at all mind having a milkshake at the White Spot on Georgia Street.

She did come to the ballpark now, at least on the nights when Bunny was starting, and she brought her friend Marilyn with her, because it would have looked a little funny, sitting there in the grandstand all alone. Bunny told her that she and Marilyn should not sit in the box seats near the dugout. He didn't want anyone to get the wrong idea.

So the night after the day on which the Ranger 4 spacecraft crashed into the moon, she saw the notorious skunk play. Bunny was pitching his best game of the season, actually, and managed a complete game shutout against the San Diego Padres, the best-hitting team in the league. The Padres pitcher was no slouch himself that evening, and lost a 1–0 game due to a spot of poor luck mixed with controversial umpiring. In the bottom of the eighth Jim Snyder, the Mounties' number seven hitter, rapped a line drive just fair down the right field line. Snyder was just slowing down around second, when he caught sight of McKeon waving frantically in the coach's box back of third. So off he went, and around third he tore, and slid beautifully across the plate.

The ball was still lying on the dewy grass just a foot or so inside fair territory and twenty feet short of the fence. The Padres right fielder was fifty feet farther into fair territory, waving his arms and kicking his feet. Standing on four feet right next to the ball, and sniffing at it with its long nose was a confident animal with lovely black fur with two white stripes along its length.

The San Diego manager and coach jumped up and down in front of the chief umpire for half an hour. They maintained that it should have been a ground rule double. The umpire avoided stepping on the caps that had been flung to the ground and repeated his opinion that there was no such ground rule regarding polecats. It may have seemed offensive, he ruled, but it was not interference.

Bunny breezed through the top of the ninth, and his record was 4–0.

Linda agreed that it would be wasteful to continue paying the rent on two apartments. Hers was close to the hospital where she supervised the kitchen, so he moved his small wardrobe in and started making friends with the mynah bird in its cage on the balcony.

He went to Seattle in her car instead of the team bus. They got their own hotel room, and she registered as "and Mrs." That was how they did things in those days. They saw just about everything there was to see in Seattle, and as game time approached he kept looking into the stands at Sick's Stadium, until he saw her abundant blonde hair and she waved at him. He took a lot of ribbing from his teammates, but that was easy to put up with. He was in love with a perfect woman and his won–lost record was at 5–0.

He beat the Rainiers 7–6 because an eighth inning two-out line drive bounced off his gluteus maximus into the bare hand of Bob Meisner, his second baseman, while the latter was falling to the ground as a result of trying to change direction, as the would-be tying run crossed the plate, and because a ninth-inning sacrifice bunt was stepped on by the would-be tying runner, causing his own put-out and converting the bunt into a single.

Bunny Watson had never been 6–0 in his life, not even as a sandlot pitcher in Boise. He did like the feeling, no doubt about that, but he was beginning to feel a little nervous. Of course he was thinking, as you are, about the leprechaun. He was a country boy from Idaho — of course he sort of believed in that sort of thing. He would never walk under a ladder or wear number 13. And he knew very well that normally an Irishman is nearly as big as a regular person.

Another thing he had never been in his life was so lucky in his love life. He knew that the Little Person had not said anything about his love life, but maybe these things always came as a package. Maybe he should have taken the pot of gold. No, he might have been able to put up with a so-so season, but could not imagine life without Linda.

"Would you love me if I was zero and six?" he asked her.

"Of course, dopey. I was nuts about you before I even knew the infield fly rule," she said.

"Dopey!" said the mynah bird.

So it went. Linda seemed to love him more and more. When he went on a long road trip that started in San Diego and proceeded northward, she waited for his return in their home that was just about exactly halfway between St. Vincent's Hospital and Capilano Stadium. When she had a day off and he had a night game, they would often enjoy a picnic at Queen Elizabeth Park, throwing bread crusts to the mallards that made large vees in the rock-ringed ponds. Once he saw a hole that must have been dug by some park animal, and imagined tiny humanoid legs sticking out of it.

Meanwhile his season proceeded steadily, from promising to good to miraculous. His ERA was more than a tad above the league average, but even reporters in other cities began to speculate about a season with no losses. In mid-May he was pulled from an error-filled game in which he had fallen behind the Salt Lake City Bees nine to one, but in the top of the ninth the usually weak-hitting Mounties rallied for eleven runs, and his loss was changed to a no-decision. Bunny felt a little funny about that one. He felt as if maybe he had *deserved* a loss.

In fact, from then on he felt as if he kind of *wanted* to lose a game, and here is why: Bunny Watson may have been a bonus baby, and he may have tried to look unbeatable on the mound, but he was one of those rare ballplayers who just love the game. Most ballplayers love *playing* the game, but Bunny loved the game for itself. The difference is a little like the difference between a baseball spectator and a baseball fan. A spectator gets all excited about a game made out of home runs and errors, a game that finishes 17–15. A fan likes a game that is 1–1 going into the ninth inning, with both starters still in. A fan is a person who would never reach down and grab a baseball that was in play and then hold it up high and look around for praise.

So Bunny Watson did not like skunks in the outfield and infielders falling on their faces. One day, when they were shopping on West Broadway, he walked under a ladder. Linda gave him a look but she didn't say anything. A few days later he spilled the salt on purpose and did nothing about it. She figured that he was just feeling the pressure of leading the league in victories.

"You were a bonus baby," she told him, and gave him a nice neck rub right there at the table. "There was a reason they gave you all that money. They knew what you were capable of."

"Hey, you want to make a bet? I'll bet you ten bucks they don't hang Adolf Eichmann."

"Heh! Why don't you bet that you'll beat the Beavers tonight?"

"I'm not due to pitch till day after tomorrow," he said.

"You're on. Ten bucks," she said.

He could see what she was up to, and she could see that he could see, and if he were to lose those ten bucks to her, as he surely would, it would be worth it.

"I'm getting to love you," he said. "I can't believe my luck."

It was the night of May 28, 1962, and you could look it up in the May 29 Vancouver *Province*, or the *Flying Saucer Review*, for all I know. The game was interesting even without the celestial fireworks toward the end. The Mounties and the Beavers, two squads with .240 team batting averages, got through the regulation nine innings without getting a runner past second base. Portland's Dante Figueroa had given up four hits, and the home team pitcher Dagoberto Cueto, one of five Cubans on the roster, had given up six hits to the visitors.

Both teams got through the tenth without incident, and there must have been a lot of real fans in attendance, because it can get cool in late May around ten at night in Vancouver. That is to say, most of the 660 witnesses were still in their seats. Forty-three of them were in possession of small containers of alcohol derived from grain.

Señor Cueto strode, as they say, out to the mound for the top of the eleventh. It was past 10:30, and the air temperature was 41°F., about 40 degrees below the temperature in Havana. He walked a Beaver. He walked a second Beaver. There were none out. Everyone in the dugout was wearing a thick jacket. It was 10:40. From then until 10:45, according to the *Vancouver Sun*, Capilano was lit up by an unearthly light.

Here are some of the things the frightful object was called: "a flaming airliner," "a burning satellite," "an off-course rocket," "a comet," and "a flying saucer."

The ballplayers took to their heels, and the six hundred folks in the stands ran for the exits. All over the city automobiles were banging into each other as drivers stuck their heads out windows. Here is what a lot of farmers and retired people in the outlying districts were thinking: "that was no meteor — someone was flying that damned thing, and it wasn't any higher than four hundred feet." Around Boise, Idaho five minutes later, people raised shotguns and rifles and opened up at the monstrous thing.

But as we know, the show must go on, the game is not over until the last man is out, etc. After a half hour of big eyes and agitated footsteps, the umpires waved the Mounties and the Portland runners back onto the field. Ron Debus left one of his bats in the on-deck circle and walked up to the plate. Everyone was set to go, two on, none out, top of the eleventh.

But there wasn't any pitcher. Jack McKeon sent the batboy and the clubhouse boy and his second string catcher to look everywhere for Bert Cueto, but it was no use. The six-foot-four-inch, 170-pound righthander from San Luis was nowhere to be found. He had either been somehow abducted by the UFO or he had a bad reaction to flaming saucers. His civilian pants and shirt were hanging on a peg in the Mounties' dressing room, but he would not be around to deal with those two base runners and Ron Debus.

The 400 fans who had come back and arranged themselves among the best seats were starting to holler suggestions. The umpires talked among themselves, then ordered McKeon to get a chucker out there or forfeit the game. McKeon looked down his bench and outside the end of the dugout, where the reliefers were sitting on kitchen chairs. No one looked back at him. All their arms were stiff. They would warm up on a night when there were no fiery objects overhead. Except for Bunny Watson. Bunny knew that he was scheduled to start the day after tomorrow, so he gave Jack a smile.

"Okay, give me an inning, Watson," said McKeon.

Bunny couldn't believe his ears, but he picked up his glove and clacked his way up the dugout steps. Under these special circumstances, the umpires were willing to give him more than the standard seven warm-up pitches. He was feeling a kind of low-level exhilaration. If he was going to give up an extra base hit and allow those runs in, they would be Bert's responsibility. If this extra and unexpected work caused some trouble during his regular turn, he might actually lose a game and feel a great deluge of relief.

He threw five fastballs and four sliders to his catcher and said he was ready. He looked at his catcher's face behind the mask as the latter made his throw to second. He thought he looked a little Irish. Well, Joe McCabe. Probably an Irish name.

He got Debus on the infield fly rule. Then Jay Hankins fouled out. Then Bill Kern flied to deep right. Three pitches.

In the bottom of the eleventh the Mounties scored the only run they needed on a two-base error and a dying quail that the second baseman heroically but tragically dived for.

Bunny got the win without breaking a sweat, and he wished that he could give it to Bert Cueto, wherever he was.

By the time of the All-Star Game in Portland July 10, Bunny's record was 14–0, with an ERA of 5.45. If it had not been for the woebegone Spokane Indians, the Mounties would be in last place. They trailed the league in batting, they were second to last (Spokane) in attendance, and in fact no one except the executives in Minneapolis knew that after the 1962 season the Mounties would be out of the league for two years. George Bamberger would be coaching for McKeon at Omaha the following year, but would go 12–12 in 1962. None of the other pitchers was anything to write home about, whether San Luis or Little Rock. In the all-star game Bunny started and got knocked out of the box in the first inning. But when Bunny got to 17–0 at home against Hawaii, there was a reporter from *Sports Illustrated* in town to do an interview to be accompanied by a few black-and-white photographs.

"To what do you attribute your amazing run?" the reporter asked, showing the acuity that got him a job with the premier sport magazine.

"Luck of the Irish," said Bunny.

"You're Irish?"

"No. My grandfather changed his name from Wojcik to Watson. My cousin John Wojcik is playing a little in the Kansas City system."

"Have the Twins said anything to you? I mean, they are not exactly pitching rich these days."

"They're looking for young guys with ERAs under 4.00. That's what I've heard."

"Can we get a picture of you on the balcony with the crow?"

"It's a mynah bird. Can you get Linda in the picture?"

"One more question. What size shoes are those?"

All through July and August there were big league scouts in Cap Stadium whenever Bunny was due to start. They were all armed with radar guns, and could be seen shaking or slapping them after Bunny had really got behind one. His fastball was still flying off in every direction, but opposing hitters were making a living off his changeup.

Bunny was more and more a creature in conflict. He knew there was something fishy about his marvelous season, and as a faithful baseball fan he was tempted to walk ten batters in a row, or toss in nothing but batting practice pitches. But he was also a competitor, and he knew that if he threw a game, he would be doing just as stinky a disservice to the great game. He could *hope* like crazy that the Tacoma cleanup hitter might get ahold of one but he had to put that ball on or just off the corner of the strike zone. Meanwhile, away from the park he "accidentally" broke a mirror, went in search of road-crossing black cats, used a single match to light three friends' cigarettes, and stepped on every crack in the sidewalk. He quit doing that when his mother wrote him from Boise about her back problems.

He read every book and article he could find about leprechauns. Most of them said that leprechauns were only
legendary or mythical creatures, and most of them mentioned pots of gold. He read James Stephens's novel *The
Crock of Gold*, but Stephens didn't know anything about
minor league baseball. One Saturday afternoon he had just
about stopped worrying about anything, because Linda
was walking around the apartment in nothing but a Vancouver Mounties cap. He was thinking about getting out
of his chair, but then he recognized the song she was humming. It was "How are things in Gloca Mora?" He felt as if
something had gone shooting by and he had just missed it.
When he looked at Linda again she was walking away, sad
and dreamy there.

What would she do if he got called up to Minnesota? She
had a good job, a really nice apartment with a view of the
mountains, and a mother and father living in Burnaby.
What would she do in Minneapolis or St. Paul, especially
when he was on the road? He almost dreaded the phone call
from the Twins. But on the other hand, which in his case
would be the right, he felt as if his 18–0 record was worth
at least a phone call.

He gave some really hard thought to the conflicting
sources of guilt and potential shame. Winning every game
because of a supernatural hex was not, well, was not *baseball*. But losing a game on purpose was actually crooked. He
was not a Black Sock. But he was not a Green Sock, either.
He decided that he would do what he could about this perfect record. One thing he did not want was to be immortal
because of that big zero. If he could lose one game the PCL
record book would be besmirched, but at least the average
baseball fan in the east would probably never hear about
the 1962 Mounties and their big-footed miracle man and
all that.

He decided that he would throw his first chance at twenty
wins. On the third of August in Hawaii, he won his nine-
teenth game when an easy fly ball bounced off outfielder

Stan Palys's chest and then resisted his frantic attempts to pick it up and throw it. "Run, run!" his teammates were hollering at Ted Sadowski, who did not get a chance to do that very often. Fall down, fall down, whispered Bunny inside his head.

Which is exactly what he did while getting off the plane in Salt Lake City four days later. McKeon had told him that he was going to start against the Bees that night. "What bad luck," said Jack, and wondered why he was getting such a big smile off his ace lefthander in his Mormon hospital bed. Next day they sent Bunny to Vancouver, where he spent three days eating the hospital food that his sweetheart had approved way back before the season opener, then three weeks sitting in an easy chair with his foot up on a pile of pillows.

"Dopey!" said the mynah.

But Linda had something nicer to say. "There are some interesting treatments I thought of while you were in the hospital," she said. "In fact, I was already thinking of them when you were in Hawaii," she said. "So now I am thinking: what better time than now to show you what I have been mulling over?"

"Mulling?"

He got back into uniform on September 1st, and threw in the bullpen to get his arm up to snuff. The main problem was making his big step, coming down on his leg, and torquing his body. His timing was all haywire at first because he flinched involuntarily when his right leg was getting ready to take the weight of his body just as the ball was leaving his left hand at 93 mph. Luckily, the Mounties played their last three series at home, against Portland, Salt Lake City and Spokane. He could work out his own timetable, throw as much as he felt able to do. One night he borrowed McKeon's radio receiver and stuck it inside his jersey. He tuned in CKWX and listened to Bobby Vinton and Neil Sedaka.

Finally, he told the skipper that he was ready to start, and on September 5th he took the mound against the Bees. It had been a few years since anyone had won twenty games in a PCL season, so there were lots of guys in hats in the stands, some with radar guns, others with wire-bound notebooks. There were also a bunch of young goons in Section 10, shouting in unison, singing loudly, throwing soft things at one another, getting off hilarious comments that no one could understand. These were university students, back in town after a summer of rigorous work in forests and packinghouses. One of them was a young George Delsing, who was wearing a terry-towel head-covering complete with long rabbit ears, an homage, one was supposed to understand, to Bunny Watson.

Neither he nor anyone else in the crowd, not even Linda Krauss, knew that Bunny intended to lose this game. In the first three innings, though, he was a bonus baby grown up. His fastball was skittery, and his slider was a hell of a surprise. The Bees batted nine men in the first three innings. No one would ever guess that this hurler was not out for champagne. In those three innings the Mounties batted twelve men, and had got two hits, one of them a single up the middle by Bunny.

After six innings it was 1–0 in favour of the home team, and the Bees had two lousy little singles. McKeon sat beside Bunny and spoke to him without taking his eyes off the field.

"Your first game back. You ready to call it a night?"

"I feel like Satchel Paige, Jack. Got an arm made of rubber and gold."

"I'll talk to you after seven," said McKeon.

After seven it was still 1–0 for the home team, and Bunny was looking for his chance. Whoever was in charge of the PA system had played "How are things in Gloca Mora" between innings. It had to be a coincidence, but time was running out. Jack might pull him at any time. In the eighth inning he threw four pitches in the dirt. He refused to look toward the dugout or the bullpen. At the end of eight it was 1–0, and he was closer to running than to walking when he assumed his place on the mound. He had breezed right by his manager. There was a righthander in the pen, up and throwing.

Ninth inning — it was his last chance to avoid that 20–0 record. The Salt Lake City Bees were a Cubs' affiliate, but there was a lot of oomph in that lineup, and its main show was up in the ninth. Walt Bond started the inning off with a sharp line drive single to left. This is my chance, thought Bunny. He pitched carefully to the slugging first baseman Tony Washington, and walked him on five pitches. Max Alvis, who had 25 home runs, surprised everyone by laying down a sacrifice bunt, and then shocked them by beating the throw to first, mainly because third baseman Julio Becquer said something loud in Cuban twice before picking up the ball.

Okay, there were three baserunners and no outs. Jack McKeon was actually standing outside the dugout, staring hard at the mound, but Bunny would not look his way. In the stands, Linda had her sweater pulled up over her eyes. George Delsing shouted, "Now you got them right where they want you, Bunny," a line he had used more than once before. No one, though, could hear him clearly, there was such a noise in the stands. A batch of Canada geese flew low over the outfield, headed vaguely southward. Jack pushed his head forward and stared harder. Bunny looked off toward Little Mountain. Those were his baserunners on those bases, so even that young guy with no name would have to have supernatural help to get his starter off the hook this time. A grin went up the side of his face opposite to the side that McKeon could see.

Now at least Salt Lake's three .300 hitters were done. Their batting order was all downhill from here. Well, the next batter was LaVern Grace, who was batting .296. He was a man of mystery, as they say. He had made the team as a walk-on halfway through the season, and would disappear from sight a week after its end. This was the guy Bunny would sacrifice to the honour of the game.

He could have just thrown the ball fifteen feet over the catcher's head, but the competitor in him would not allow such a big margin. Bunny did his best to avoid thought, and before he knew it, the count was 3–2. Delsing turned to the guy standing beside him in Section 10 and shouted, "Three on, a 3–2 count, the next pitch is always a foul ball."

Okay, Bunny decided to make this pitch good and ambiguous. He went high and in, not exactly a beanball, but up enough and in enough to make a married man pee. It was his famous fastball with the tail. It started off looking like a strike, and then veering toward LaVern's left eye. LaVern tried to swing and fall on his ass at the same time.

What happened then took less time than this is going to take to tell you what happened then. First the baseball came into contact with a bat that was being moved three directions at once. Then the baseball travelled in a very slight arc to a spot midway between second base and the spot that the shortstop, in this case Jose Valdevielso, normally will occupy. Señor Valdevielso reached up with his glove and caught the ball, retiring Mr. Grace, and a few steps later touched second base with his left shoe, thus putting out Mr. Washington, who could not get back fast enough, then kept running until he had reached Mr. Alvis, who had fallen down in his attempt to stop his progress toward second and attempt to return to the bag where he belonged. Jose V. reached down and tapped Max's leg with his glove.

Actually, this all happened about like this: You're Out! You're Out! You're Out!

Then Jose realized what he had just done. An unassisted triple play. Then Bunny realized what had happened. He was twenty and nothing. One by one the Mounties figured it out, and raced toward Valdevielso to jump on him and give him a congratulatory squeeze. All except their winning pitcher, who hung his head and walked as fast as he could toward the dugout and the dressing room behind it. There were two pictures in the *Sun* next day: one showed ballplayers in a pile, the other a non-celebrating walker. The caption suggested that the latter was in shock.

All that day the telephone rang in the apartment, and every time Bunny picked it up, the mynah bird said, "Hello?"

"Here's what I can't figure out," said Bunny, when Linda came home from work. "I get about a hundred calls since six this morning, and not one of them is from the Twins. While I'm at it, I also can't figure out how come they didn't call me up a month ago."

"It *is* odd, isn't it?" Linda replied. "I mean they're going to finish second."

He could not help smiling. She was keeping track of the American League standings. A year ago she had probably never heard of the Minnesota Twins. He felt lucky in love.

"Maybe," she said, "the Twins just never heard about what you have been doing this season."

"Or what's been done *to* me."

"Ah, that's crazy. The whole world knows, don't they?"

"Unless this is all a dream."

"So *I'm* dreaming too?"

"Maybe *you* are a dream."

Now he was getting a little scared.

"You know, I won't believe the numbers till I read the record books five years from now. And I *am* glad to be 20–0. I would rather be 20–0 than 4–18. But I would rather be, I don't know, 14–7. I kind of wish that I had taken the pot of gold instead."

The evening of September 9 would see the last Mounties game in Vancouver until 1965, and the last outing on the mound for their astonishing pitcher, Bunny Watson. The visitors were the cellar-dwelling Spokane Indians, who had already lost 96 games, and were not expecting to do much against Mr. Perfect. Bunny was thinking what the hell, the Russians have agreed to send missiles to Cuba, and we could all be ashes in another few weeks, we and all our records. He was just going to use his fastball all night, and see what happened.

There was a towel over something in his locker. Oh boy, his teammates were pulling something. But when he gingerly removed the towel, this is what he saw: a miniature kettle pot with one gold coin inside. He grinned while getting dressed. He put the coin in his pants pocket for luck. Then he grinned while taking his warm-up pitches. Then he went out and pitched nine innings and got whacked by the Indians 8–0.

He was still grinning when he joined his fiancée in the players' parking lot.

"What is your real name?" he asked her.

"Iris," she said.

☐ Alison and the Rest

Alison had been wearing quite a lot more makeup since Edgar had betrayed her. That's what she called it, betrayed her. What we know is that Edgar had just stopped telephoning her, and then began appearing at parties and the like with another woman, and then another, and eventually the most recent one, Lenora, seemed to stick. We were friends of both Alison and Edgar, so we could not just turn our backs on either of them. But Alison, with more and more makeup on her face, with her own eyebrows shaved off and new ones pencilled in as if she were a dowager in a thirties movie, became importunate. Is that a word?

Barry used to be in love with Alison, hopeless love, and maybe he still is. I say hopeless love because Alison would rather take abuse from Edgar than undiluted adoration from Barry. It's not that Barry is unattractive. Except for his awful hair, he is a presentable enough looking man for his height. He told me once that he wanted to cause harm to Edgar. He said that if Edgar darted in front of his car he would not hit the brake. I guess some of us would.

Cathy would have been one of those. She had had a crush on Edgar ever since she had turned twelve. She was thirteen when Edgar betrayed Alison, but Edgar was forty-one. Of course being thirteen, Cathy could not drive a car anyway. But she took every opportunity that showed its face to get into Edgar's car, a perfectly ordinary Toyota Corolla. Edgar just thought of her as Lenora's little sister, poor thing. It never entered his head that a thirteen-year-old girl with buck teeth could have sexual fantasies.

Dennis, well you know Dennis, I guess. Apparently he was the person who deprived Alison of her virginity way back when. Okay, that would be fine. But Dennis had a way of reminding everyone, especially Alison, especially Alison and especially Edgar, if you can have two especiallies. Not long before Edgar betrayed Alison he beat the shit out of Dennis. Hooray, thought a lot of people. Oh no, the bastard, thought the rest of us. No one knows what Alison said to him, but we didn't think that she stuck up for herself enough.

Edgar was really good-looking—you had to give him that. His hair was thick and curly and shiny black. His nose was straight. He had a strong jaw. His ears did not stick out, the way mine do. He was about five foot ten in his black loafers. He could have had just about any young woman in our crowd, and did have quite a few of them. He never seemed to love them, really. He saved his love for himself and whatever snazzy car he was driving at the time. Alison was not the first sweet thing he had dumped without informing, but she was the first to say that he had betrayed her.

Fiona was better looking than Edgar, though, so we were all tickled when he tried to pick her up and she flipped him off. Your place or mine? he asked her at the Domino one night. I take it that your place is the reptile cage at the zoo, she said, one eyelid up. I do not attend zoos. Edgar took Alison home that night. The way she told it to Grace, he was a thoughtful lover. She knew that Grace would tell Fiona. For some reason Alison had it in for Fiona.

Grace and I were pretty good friends and had been so since we'd met at art school. Once in a while we would fall into bed and make love, but tacitly we agreed that it would be a friendly pleasure we gave each other and took from each other rather than a commitment about the future. If I was ever going to fall in love with anyone it would be Alison, but I was smart enough to know that that was not going to get me anywhere. So I had a drink or a coffee with her best friend and took her best friend's clothes off from time to time.

Hal was an old-fashioned boy. He thought that women would fall in love with him for his athletic skills. He looked at the advertisements in sports magazines and saw beautiful blondes crawling on jocks with grass stains on their clothing. But he was also in love, not only with himself, but seriously, in love with Fiona. He noticed that Fiona carried a book wherever she went, but he thought that meant that she did not have a proper lover to occupy her time. Whatcha readin'? he once asked her, to break the ice. Derrida, she replied. He dropped the subject.

I gave Alison a shoulder to lean on, and then I smoothed her hair and gave her a kiss on the forehead. She pushed herself harder against me, and I could, I know, I could have gone all the way with her. But I was romantic and noble. These are the words I use to make fun of myself. I did give her a kiss on the lips, but quickly, deftly, as if saying I am only a kind of old friend who wants to protect or comfort you.

Janine complicated things quite a bit, because though she was married to Mark, she too had the hots for Alison. Maybe I shouldn't use that language. She too had a crush on Alison. You could tell from the way she handed Alison a cupcake at her birthday party. Janine once told me to quit my hopeless mooning about Alison. When I said that maybe I should make a move on Mark, she actually slapped my face.

Keith had the hots for Hal. There is no better way to describe that. Hal had a body that was a result of daily working out in the gym. He, like his friends, called it working out because they wanted their activity to resemble work. Or to seem to resemble it. I remember, as a kid, seeing the kind of muscles my father and others got from working, and they were a lot different from the muscles Hal and his friends had. Keith

did not have much in the way of muscles. He would run to
catch a bus, but that was about the extent of his athletic life.
He never told Hal about his interest in Derrida.

Lenora did everything she could do to make Edgar happy.
You could tell that she was an inexperienced young woman.
It got so that Edgar told her what clothes to wear to the
bar or parties. She had probably never shown so much skin
in her life. The more makeup Alison wore, the more skin
Lenora showed. It got so that we felt as if we couldn't look
at her. At one party Alison spent the whole night in the
bathroom, and everyone had to go to the basement can or
out in the yard.

Mark and I always seemed to be interested in the same
woman. I was supposed to be his best friend, but I was
always filled with resentment or something, not resentment, exactly, but a feeling that ate like stomach acid at
the edges of our friendship. I don't know whether he felt the
same way. When I went to bed with Grace he started flirt-
ing with her. So I flirted with his wife. Janine had no idea
what it was about.

Nora was having sex with as many people in our set as
she could get into bed or out in the weeds or on the roof, for
all I know. I will admit that she added me to her list, but I
was a little drunk and angry at the time. As far as I know,
she preferred men, but I know that she made it with Grace
and Sierra. She once asked me whether I would like to do
a double with her and young Cathy. You'll give us all a bad
name, I told her.

Olivia was Edgar's mother, but I swear, she must have
been fifteen when he was born. We didn't know whether to
treat her as someone from the generation before us or as just
part of our circle, I guess you'd call it. If she and Edgar were
in the same room, she would be picking lint off his jacket
or correcting his pronoun usage. Olivia told Alison she was
lucky to have gotten away with all her teeth intact.

Peter and Warren were a gay couple who did not live
together. "I'm the Mia Farrow person here," Warren would

sometimes say. "But he has not adopted any children," Peter would add. Nora tried to get them interested in a bedroom threesome, apparently, but I think she was joking. Cathy was an entirely different story. Being thirteen and unconcerned with consequences, she turned on all her adolescent charm every time she ran into Peter. Then Edgar would shake his fist at Peter.

Quinn said she had just about had it with Alison. Remember that I said Alison was getting more and more importunate. It got so that she was begging people to talk with Edgar, remonstrate with him for betraying her, urge him to take her back. Once Alison and Quinn went to a serious French movie together, and after they came out Alison jumped off the first bridge they came to. Luckily, one supposes, it was a very low bridge. All she got was a twisted ankle and dirty clothes.

Roberto had somewhere picked up the notion that his Spanish accent and Latin-style good looks would get him just about anywhere with the gringo ladies. Well, he did have black flashing eyes and thick shiny black hair. Light just seemed to bounce off him everywhere. He took it on himself to comfort Alison, but when he tried to segue from comfort into heavy petting, as they used to say in the youth magazines, she told Hal, and Hal flexed his muscles at Roberto.

Sierra did make it with Nora, but as with all things concerning Nora, it was in no way serious. I asked Sierra whether she would be so kind as to put in a good word for me with Alison. She said it had been a long time since she had had a good word to give. Then can you tell her to stop it with the makeup, I asked. She isn't thirteen years old, I added. Also, I added, could you tell Lenora to cover a little more skin. There are more UV rays coming from this group than you can shake a stick at.

Tannis is a folksinger, so we have all learned to take whatever she says with a grain of sea salt. There's that, and then there's the way she uses us. It wasn't long after Edgar's betrayal of Alison that Tannis was strumming her dulcimer and singing a song about it. I feel like smashing her goddamned autoharp, said Olivia. Dulcimer, I said. Whatever, she said. You are an overprotective mother, I said. No, I feel like doing it for Alison, she said. Tannis looked at us as if she wanted us to join in the song.

Ulrich would make fun of Barry's appearance every chance he got. The rest of us would tell Polish jokes with Ulrich as the protagonist or at least the audience. Why do so many Polish people have badly burned ears? But Ulrich would also make jokes about Alison. That is what led to the incident with the bowling trophy. It was kind of ironic in a way, what with there being so many Polish guys in the bowling alley around that time. We made sure that Barry didn't walk home by himself for a while after that.

Vicki always knew just what anyone needed to fix them up. She let Keith tell her all about Derrida and the idea of the "trace," I think it was at the time. She once gave me a tug job in a darkened car when I particularly needed some human contact. She kept taking Alison to some chichi tea house for herbal chai. She didn't ask her how she had acquired a black eye that one morning in April. When Alison let herself weep a little, Vicki went at her with a Kleenex and took the opportunity to get some of the extra makeup off. Vicki, I told her, you could have been a great social worker. I'm a social *system*, she said.

Wallace was only a dog — I mean literally. Not "only" a dog, you might say, because he was an enormous and very fat basset hound. Honestly, I do not know who his purported owner was. He just seemed to be around, at any number of houses, so you did not know whether he was an incumbent or a visitor. Now this is unpleasant — he liked to lie on his back under the table, his distended pink belly topped by his huge dog penis. It was not total pleasure to be having a summer luncheon with that snuffling dog lying on his back under the table.

X was the name Warren was going by that summer. We don't know why, exactly, but it might have had something to do with the interest everyone was taking in the battle for Gay Rights. You don't have to spell it with a capital letter, Peter would always say. Maybe you Uncle Scotts don't, but some of us are going on the offensive. Honestly, Peter, sometimes I could mistake you for a breeder. That was the term that summer. You are wearing eye makeup, aren't you, said Peter. Honestly, you are looking more and more like Alison.

Yolanda did not speak more than thirty words of English, but she made up for that with her enthusiasm and her long fingernails. She would put her arm around Alison and coo at her in some Mediterranean language, and Alison would let a tear fall from her eye, through her pancake makeup and onto her lap. On one occasion Edgar called her a name we didn't understand, but no one's respect for Edgar grew just because he could say a nasty word he probably picked up in a foreign bar. I was not all that much of a Yolanda fan, but the skin on my back crawled when I saw her fingernails.

Zoë told me what was going to happen. Zoë is a mystery writer, so she knows how to size these things up. She said that Edgar and Barry would be the prime suspects. Prime in the sense that they would be the first two everyone would think of, except, of course, for them and the real killer. I asked her to tell me more, to at least give me a hint. I have no informati spare, she said.

☐ Sworn to Secrecy

I was sworn to secrecy about this, but that was a long time ago, and I am not absolutely certain that the people who swore me to secrecy actually had the power and authority to swear me. Power, maybe, but I am not so sure about authority. In that situation it was and is a little hard to define authority.

It doesn't really matter anyway, because here I go.

I was still a writer back then. Well, I suppose that I didn't have any more right to call myself a writer then than I do now, now that I have quit. I mean by that that I had done a lot of writing, but I had not had anything published. Except for some poems; anyone can get their poems published in this country.

I had sat at my portable Underwood and written three and a half novels, mostly about growing up and trying to make it in the world. But then I decided to write a detective novel. I figured that if you can write a detective novel, you can write any kind of novel. Detective novels are strong on plot, of course, I mean ha ha, and also strong on setting and character and suspense and all those things that everyone knows you need in a story.

I always figured that if you want to write a western, you should go and ride a horse for a while. If you figure on a historical novel, read everything about the time and go visit the place. If you intend to write skin books, do your research. I was planning a detective novel. I decided to follow someone. I got myself one of those little green shirt-pocket notebooks with the coil and a good waterproof pen. I already had a miniature tape recorder — well, it was miniature for those days. I considered a trench coat and Humphrey Bogart hat, but decided against them. I didn't want to look like a cartoon character. I wanted to blend in with the background, eh?

How did I pick someone to follow? I just took a bus downtown, got off at Robson Street, and lit up a Sportsman, bending toward the matchbook flame cupped in my hands. When I looked up, I saw a guy in a dark blue suit and open dark blue trench coat. Perfect. He was carrying a furled black umbrella in one hand and a black attaché case hung from the other. It was as if I had put in an order. I let the cigarette dangle from the left corner of my mouth and with my hands in my jacket pockets, walked about a quarter of a block behind the guy.

I took notes in my head so that I could transfer them to my notebook when I had a chance. They would eventually be material for my novel if I was lucky and this worked out. I was a writer following a — well, I didn't know what he was, but he looked like a business guy, maybe in insurance, maybe in the prosecutor's office. According to my notes he was about forty or forty five years old, wore glasses with rims on the top only, had conservative sideburns and hair that must have been cut in the past four days. There was a blue thread hanging from the hem of his trench coat in back, and a line of light grey mud around his black leather shoes. I figured he must have parked his car in an unpaved lot.

There was no music. This was real life or something to read.

I hung behind him as he walked west on Robson Street, making sure I caught the walk signals he caught, then hanging back, smoking my cigarette like a detective. He

went into a little corner grocery (remember, this was back
before Robson Street had become a franchise strip mall)
and bought some Smith Brothers cough drops. I was close
enough to see that the flavour was Wild Cherry, and wondered whether a private eye was supposed to figure out
something from that, or whether it was even supposed to
show up in his notes.

Private eye or police gumshoe? Maybe I ought to write a
spy novel, I thought. Just take notes and lurk, I told myself,
make the narrative decision later. I wished that I had
brought a hat so I could pull it down over my face. This following a guy was fun.

He turned right on Burrard and before I knew it he was
downstairs at the pub in the Hotel Vancouver, and so was I.
I tried to look as if I were meeting someone, looking around
and letting my eyes adjust to the dim light. I wanted to
make sure that he sat down before I did. He sat at a round
terry cloth table and waited for a man with a tray of beer. I
did likewise, and took out the paperback book I was reading,
The Confidential Agent by Graham Greene. I pretended to
read it, and then pretty soon I was reading it. I hardly took
my eyes off the page as I paid for my beer, and I gave only a
fleeting glance to my subject, who was sipping his beer and
reading something typed on a sheaf of papers.

Once you start on a Graham Greene book, it's hard to
make yourself stop for a while. The waiter was asking me
whether I wanted another one, and the man I was interested in was gone. I jumped out of my seat, knocking the
table with my hip, and walked fast to the steps and up to
the street.

I didn't see him in any direction.

"Did you see a guy with an umbrella and a briefcase?" I
asked a guy with a newspaper and a briefcase.

"Piss off, joker," he replied.

I decided to look along Georgia Street, and it was a good
thing (I thought then) that I did, because a block later I
looked to the west, and there he was, waiting at the bus

stop for the 444. Aha, I thought, so he's going to the north shore. Very interesting, I said to myself. I was still trying to get into the role. I took my place at the back of the lineup.

Two cigarettes later the bus was there, and I was the last to climb on board. It was packed, so I didn't have much choice about where to sit. As it turned out I was right behind my subject. He just sat there all the way, a forty-minute ride through the park and over the bridge and back east toward downtown North Vancouver, if there was such a thing back then. He got off at the main drag, and so did I, making sure that I was the last off.

And when I looked, he had disappeared.

I walked back and forth, looking into stores, checking parked cars, staring as far as I could up the hill and down. I looked down eight side streets. I was out of breath, hurrying uphill and not stopping to rest. I was a spy with a panic attack. I had lost him. The free world was going to slip further into calamity.

Not to mention the fact that it was a long ride back to town, and I was out double bus fare.

Here is where a sensible person, or let's say just about anyone, would quit and just make things up, or start following someone else who didn't go over to the north shore. But not me. I was always like that back then. I had to stick with the plan.

All this was being financed by my unemployment insurance cheque; I had breathed a little too much overheated air in a factory fire four months before, and now in the last days of December, I still could not be trusted to breathe my way through a day's work. With the plant gone, the work would be mainly cleaning up and rebuilding, but I didn't have any carpenter's papers. I was a lifter and carrier, and here at the rainy end of the year I still felt it when I lifted my raincoat.

Nope, I had to continue with the guy I had picked at random, if that is what it was, though a briefcase and an umbrella might have suggested something. I went back to Robson and Granville the next day and lit a cigarette and tried to look like a young spy without a hat.

He didn't show up. I went to the Plaza Theatre and saw a movie, *The Manchurian Candidate*. It was about guns and espionage and people in over their heads. I took notes in the dark of the theatre.

I lucked out the next afternoon, a Wednesday on the Pacific shore. There I was, on the corner of Howe and Robson, and along he came, wearing the same outfit, with his trench coat open and its long belt flipping back and forth as he strode westward. The sidewalks and streets were wet, but it was no longer raining, and until the early darkness, slices of silvery sun had been showing through the rolled clouds. Neon lights shone in the puddles. I stuck my Sportsman in the left corner of my mouth, stuck my hands in my coat pockets, and followed a guy whose name I did not know, west along Robson. He ducked into the little store, but he didn't buy cough drops this time. He must have been feeling better. This time he bought a package of Drum pipe tobacco and stuffed it into one of his big pockets.

Then off it was again to the basement beverage room of the Hotel Vancouver. He sat at a different table this time, and ordered a glass of beer. I sat and opened my book and ordered a glass too. This time I was going to make sure I was watching when he got up to go. Twice when I looked up from Graham Greene, the guy's eyes met mine. I pretended that I didn't register.

I got onto the bus last again, and had to sit way in the back, but I could see him all right. I can't read on the bus without getting nauseated, but I took out *The Confidential Agent* and pretended to read it. When he got out at Lonsdale I was ready, and when he turned off Lonsdale and walked east on 4th Street it was dark but I was on him. He walked into a little white stucco house second from the corner, and pretty soon lights went on in three or four rooms. Now

I knew where he lived, if this was his house, and it looked as if he either lived all alone or his family was somewhere else for the present.

"Surveillance," I said to myself. Now what?

I walked around to the lane just to see what I could see, and had to duck when a light went on over his back door. There he was with a wastebasket in either hand, coming down the steps. It must have been garbage pickup eve in North Van. I found the darkest spot I could, and watched him while he lifted the lid of his battered aluminum garbage can, dumped in the contents of the two wastebaskets, jammed the lid on tight because North Van is full of raccoons, and dragged the garbage can to the edge of the lane. He went back inside, but he left the back light on.

Now I knew what I was going to do next.

I lifted the battered lid carefully, remembering in a flash that when we were kids playing knights and Saracens, we used garbage can lids for shields, a bad idea, because all the banging of a Saracen sword on your garbage can lid was made known to the knuckles of your bare left hand, and now here I was playing a more up-to-date game, but trying to be quiet because there was just a little too much light there in the lane behind 4th Street East. As the bottommost garbage had presumably been in the can for just about a week, there was a nasty odour, but on top of the putrefied stuff was a pile of discarded paper, some of it brochures, and some of it envelopes. I was, of course, interested in the envelopes.

In less than a minute I was pretty sure I knew my subject's name and address. I put the lid back on the garbage can as quietly as any spy could, and slid an envelope into my jacket pocket.

Now what do I do, I asked myself during the time it took to fall into sleep that night. I know his name. I know where he lives. I know where he goes after work. But where does he work? I couldn't very well follow him backward in time, though I thought about writing the kind of story in which

I could do that. But I had dedicated myself to learning how to write a spy story or at least a mystery, definitely not a science fiction story. Still, it was a pretty nifty idea, and it would solve the problem of finding out where Mr. Quarry spent his days. The other way would be to get up early and scoot over to North Van and follow him into town.

Just before I fell asleep, I think, I wondered this to myself: If you were training to become a science fiction writer, wouldn't that mean that in the real world you could find a way to research time travel, at least enough to follow Mr. Quarry back a block or two, a minute or two, to his workplace? In the morning that didn't sound right, and even now, decades later, it doesn't sound right, but there is something there, isn't there?

What could I do? I couldn't pick him up earlier in his routine, because all I had was what I got in that first impulsive decision to follow him from the corner of Granville and Robson. I should have picked up some subject in the building he worked in. I could start over with a new subject. But no, if I were going to be a detective, or at least write about being a detective, I had to detect, damn it. I would make a more thorough search of his place, find out what magazines he subscribed to, who wrote letters that he cared enough about to save, where he worked, maybe. I would never get all this stuff from going through his garbage. It would require being inside his little white house.

I thought about the procedure all the way there on the 444 bus. First I would try the basement door and the basement windows. A lot of people didn't bother locking their basement windows. If that didn't work out, I would have to consider making a little windowpane break. I could leave some money to pay for a new windowpane. How much was a windowpane worth, I mean including the guy who has to replace it, I mean if the subject himself didn't know how to do it. I was a detective with a very small bankroll. Five dollars was nearly a week's food. Ten dollars was out of the question.

When I got to Mr. Quarry's block I took a little walk, round and round the block, in all possible directions. It was a normal December day in North Vancouver, heavy clouds spilling down the mountain forest, forlorn seagulls screeching in the distance. Everything was very quiet in this neighbourhood at one thirty in the afternoon. I could walk more than a block without a car going by.

I saw no activity at all in his block. I walked the length of his back lane, and was on the edge of walking back to his place, when I thought: what if someone looking out her lace-edged kitchen door sees me walking up and down her lane? So I took another little walk, and then entered the lane for a slow but not overly slow pace almost to the other end. There were two vehicles parked quiet and empty, a paint-chipped Morris Minor at one end of the block, and a dirty mustard-coloured panel van a couple doors from Mr. Quarry's cottage.

Right in the middle of my bony chest I could hear my heart banging as I went into the little back yard with its dead flower stalks. I tried to make it look as if I had a reason to be there, in case any neighbour was watching. I stepped right up onto the short porch and reached for the doorknob, and the door just opened up before me, without a creak or a groan. I stepped inside, of course — who wouldn't, spy or spy novelist or none of the above. There was just about as much light in the kitchen as there was in the yard. Until, that is, everything disappeared because there was a bag of some sort pulled over my head.

I was being grabbed and pushed against a counter, and someone shoved me to my knees, and I could not move my arms or see anything, and there was a horrible smell or taste inside that bag or whatever it was, something chemical or rotting, something that could have been potatoes liquefied with age, could have been neglected bivalves. I was not try- ing to escape — I was trying to breathe and stay vertical in a sense, though on my knees. It seemed as if there were three of them, though it could have been two.

They hauled me to my feet and yanked the bag down over my shoulders and arms, and pushed me the way they wanted me to go. They may have been talking to me or to each other, but all I could hear was a number of mouth sounds. I felt myself pushed out the door and off the porch. It was all I could do to stay on my feet. Then I heard another sound, and I was pushed and lifted roughly, and then I was lying down, and then an engine started and we were moving. I figured this out — I was lying down on the dirty metal floor of that mustard-coloured van. One of the kidnappers was sitting on me.

After a lot of lefts and rights and downhills and uphills, the van came to a stop, and the driver came back and helped sit on me for a while. One of the guys made some pretty loud mouth sounds, probably, and then the other one did too, and then back to the first one and so on. I could tell that they were not just having a conversation, because each time they shouted something I couldn't hear, one of them would kick me. I don't think they were trying for my nuts, but just desiring to make a point.

So I made some mouth sounds back at them. I was sort of saying words, as far as I was concerned, saying something along the lines of "will you guys please stop kicking me and take this smelly thing off my head?" But to them, I am sure, it just sounded like mouth sounds they could not understand. Things were quiet for a minute. Then they turned me on my stomach on the ridged metal of the van's floor, and slowly pulled the horrible bag off my head. Just when it was coming totally off, one of them pushed my face down hard on the metal.

"Hold still, Partner," is what he said.

Partner? I had not heard that kind of sobriquet since our family visits to Quesnel when I was a pre-teener.

Then someone was tying a filthy cloth around my head in such a way as to make it impossible for me to see anything, including the filthy cloth. It smelled like old suppurating crankcase oil.

"Okay, listen hard, Partner." And he gave me a slap to the side of my head. "You're going to answer some questions."

"Why are you slapping me around?" I enquired.

"Because we can," said the other guy, and it was presumably he who grabbed me and sat me up and slapped me on the back of the head.

"I would never have deigned to write a scene like this," I muttered.

"What?" Slap.

"First question," said the other guy.

"Delsing. George Delsing," I said.

"We *know* your name, asshole. You think we're chumps?"

"Is that the first question?"

That was a stupid, really stupid thing to say, but I could not help myself. I was scared silly, but I was also finding this hard to believe. They kicked me and slapped my head harder than ever.

"Who are you working for?" asked the one I was thinking of as the first guy.

"I am unemployed. I am getting twenty-four dollars a week of Unemployment Insurance."

Four kicks. Four slaps. One little finger bent back hard.

"Oh, you mean *this*, this back alley business."

"Yes, this back alley *business*. Who?"

"I'm not working for anyone. Not working at all."

"You go to a lot of trouble following people and casing their place and all that, for someone who isn't working."

I did not like the edge of petulance that had crept into the second guy's voice. Petulance under anger is not pleasant to hear. It sounds dangerous.

"Well, in a sense, I am working for myself." I could hear a loud ringing in my ears. "I'm thinking about writing a book — "

"Yeah, everyone's thinking of writing a book," said the first guy. "Do they all go stulking in back alleys?"

"Skulking."

"What?"

"Skulking. You said stulking. It's skulking."

"That's what I said, skulking."

"That's what he said, Gumball," said the second guy, and spit on my neck. When I reached up to wipe it off with my sleeve, he punched me under the arm, hard.

I decided that I had better let it go, and anything else that came up.

"I was thinking of writing a spy book, or something like that, maybe a detective book, where the guy has to find out stuff about a stranger."

"You're a spy planning on writing a book."

"No no. The other way around."

"You're a book planning on writing a spy?"

"Well, that's closer."

That concession earned me four slaps across the face.

"And it's whom," I said, with a little blood on my bottom lip.

"What the fug are you talking about?" was the reply, because this was 1962.

"You asked who I was working for. Should have been whom."

Now they banged me around without benefit of questions or other spoken words for a while. They did grunt during a kick, and one of them whistled lightly through his teeth while banging my head. I considered losing consciousness, but could not do so. It came to me, though, that they were wordlessly pounding on me because they believed my story about being a future novelist and were experiencing frustration.

They stopped for a while to smoke cigarettes. I was hurting all over, and now persuaded that this was really happening. So I asked the question that had just entered my mind.

"Am I going to get a cigarette?"

"No."

"So for whom are you folks working?"

"Don't worry about it," said the first guy.

"Because, I have been thinking about it, taking advantage of the situation, you might say, and it came to me that maybe you guys are doing the same thing."

"Clarify your point, Partner."

"How do I know that you are real kidnappers?"

"We are not kidnappers. We are something you don't know about."

"How do I know you are real whatevers, real spies, private detectives, whatever?" I licked blood off the side of my mouth.

One of them gave me a fist to my left ear.

"Does that feel real?" he asked.

"Be reasonable," I urged. "I have experience of myself as a pretend spy or private detective, so you can see why it might enter my mind that you guys are much the same. I mean how do I know that you guys are, say, real operatives?"

"Ha!" said the second guy.

"How do we know that you are a fake one?"

"Oh, I'm fake."

"Because if you are real and we let you off without getting the information from you . . . I am sure you can see our predicament."

"Well, from the easy way you snaffled me, I would have to say that either I am a very poor operative, or I am a fake one, trying to figure out how to write a spy story."

They conferred, apparently. I could hear them whispering behind hands somewhere in the van.

"We are inclined to believe that you are a phony," said the first guy.

"Fake," I offered.

"So we are going to make you an author. We can tie you up and fasten you to a block of concrete we already have in this vehicle for such contingencies, and deposit you in nearby Burrard Inlet, or we can swear you to secrecy with the information that we know where you live, etcetera."

"You're going to make me an author?"

"What are you talking about?"

"You said you were going to make me an author."

"Offer. I said we are making you an offer."

"You said author."

"Listen, you stupid dork, do you want me to tie you to our block of concrete?"

Needless to say, I chose to be sworn to secrecy. And I have never mentioned the event to anyone until now. In fact, I had sort of forgotten about it. It was just that a couple of nights ago I was listening to the radio, and they were doing election coverage, talking to candidates and voters and back room boys, and I heard a familiar voice. People's voices don't change much, even while their faces and bodies are looking older all the time. After casting around in my memory for a few seconds, I knew who it was to whom I was listening. It was the first guy in the van that night.

Maybe I shouldn't be telling anyone about all this, but what the hell — if you are ever going to start being a writer, you have to quit burying things in the dirt, or the Inlet, say.

☐ Phyllis's Questions

Listen. If I have known beauty
let's say I came to it
asking

I. At the Conference

It was the end of the first night. Everyone had to get up at some ungodly hour in the morning, and we were the only two people from the conference still in the bar. She was smoking. I was trying not to.

"It looks to me as if your work is becoming more and more influential on the younger poets. They say your name all the time, now," I said.

"Oh, who can tell the apparent from the real?"

"Well, you simply have to look at the magazines and books. The dedications of poems. The interviews in which poets say that you opened the way for them."

"And when is the apparent not the real?"

"I suppose there are times when poets and others say things that on closer examination don't carry any substance. But you've had whole issues of magazines devoted to your work, for example."

I felt an urge toward formal syntax. Probably because she was not exactly using bar room language herself.

"And who would cleave the apparent from the real?"

"Really, you hardly ever see such a wave of warm feelings. They love you. You must know that."

"Or now shall we kiss where once we laughed?"

"I don't think anyone ever laughed about you." I tilted ice cubes against my teeth. "There was that one reviewer who complained about the price that poor book buyers had to pay for all the white space in *Naked Poems*. But he's been buried, I think."

"Head up, head down?"

I liked it better when the tone became light. Well, with her it was never loose and light. But there were levels of irony, some more comfortable than others.

"Head down, I would think. Screwed into the ground. I imagine that he gets tired of looking at worms and reflecting on the fecklessness of his opinion."

"Knows the irrelevance of defeat?"

"Not so much that he was defeated, or beheaded. He just spent his life without learning how to review a book."

"How to release without injury?"

"You're nobody's fish, my sweet, and there was no injury, as far as I can see, though you are well known for the elegance of your suffering. But that's enough about negative responses. I was talking about love."

I was always a little afraid of approaching this subject. So I always rushed into it. The whole interior of the bar was reflected in the windows that during the day offered a wonderful view of two rivers converging. I looked at the windows rather than the woman with the mauve silk at her throat.

"Oh my darling, tell me, what can love mean in such a world, and what can we or any lovers hold in this immensity of hate and broken things?"

I had learned to stay in my chair when she suddenly shifted the level. Sometimes irony just plain disappeared, and I did not have a lot of experience with what filled its place. I kept my eyes on the windows.

"Come on, now, poet. You may not be a fishwoman, but you are Neptune's daughter. You hang out on the rocky shore, looking at the water collected in Wilson's bowl. You were there when the old god sent a regatta of love for your own eyes. You wrote us a lot of lovely island poems. You were in your element and Neptune was smiling on you. He's a pretty good world in himself."

"Or, was it through waves he sent the boats to fly with gulls so that out of care they all could play in a wonderful gull-boat-water way up in a land of air?"

She was waving her long cigarette, a sign that light irony was back. I managed to look at her again. My, she looked good. It was pretty near closing time, so I signalled for a couple more, and for once it worked.

"You made us see all that, lady," I said.

"Oh, who can tell the apparent from the real?"

"Apparently they can be the same thing."

"And when is the apparent not the real?"

"I guess when some logician is at work, rather than — ahem — a protean island poet."

I was pretty well enjoying this, and I think she was, too, though that is an entirely different thing.

"And who would cleave the apparent from the real?"

"Not I, not ever I. I would not be able to look you in the face, for example, were I to try that. You are the poet of love, not the examiner of the real, I would have to say."

She leaned forward and put three fingers on the tweed that covered my forearm.

"Oh my darling, tell me, what can love mean in such a world, and what can we or any lovers hold in this immensity of hate and broken things?"

Up, down, up, down. I decided to be the voice of late night stability.

"I was not aware that we were lovers," I said. "Not even in the literary sense. Not even in a world piled high with broken things. I know that you know that nature is still to be found, even the nature depicted in art. It is still there, even in this world with its adequate supply of hate. Especially up here among these clear hills."

"When will the caribou come?"

She was sitting back, looking at the window, as if she could see the river outside.

"I beg your pardon."

"When will the caribou come?"

"That look in your eyes, Woman. You could be an Inuit, starving in the snow fields."

"What has Jack Hornby come for?"

Oh, him.

"Even our friend George Whalley could never solve that riddle," I said. "But he performed something more important. He was able to place us right in the middle of his folly, in the hopeless impossibility of the north that Hornby challenged in his madness. The consequence of his pride, if that is what it was. We are left asking questions that will not be answered but only repeated."

I should be saving this for tomorrow's panel discussion, I thought.

"When will the caribou come — I don't mean to stay — but when will they come?"

"I don't know."

"When will the caribou come?"

"I don't think they will be here this year."

"When will they come?"

"They are not going to come, I'm afraid. Hornby knew that was possible."

"Oh, when will they come!"

"You will never see them."

"But when will the caribou come?"

"Oh, Phyllis. If that is who you are."

"When will they come to eat from my hand?"

"Only after we are all gone, dear one."

"Knowing that everything is wrong, how can we go on giving birth either to poems or the troublesome lie, to children, most of all, who sense the stress in our distracted wonder the instant of their entry with their cry?"

I knew when it was time to meet her seriousness. It was one of the thousand things I loved her for.

"Maybe this world needs them more than ever. Remember Doc Williams wrote that every day people die for the lack of what is to be found in poems."

"But I, how can I, I, craving the resolution of my earth, take up my little gang of sweet pretence and saunter day-dreary down the alleys, or pursue the half-disastrous night?"

"Now I am led two ways. That is honestly beautiful, the way you put that. And I believe the intensity of your despair — is that a good term? But it also seems that your gift for speaking so well, your work as a poet, is the very thing that can redeem you — and the damned world."

She made me talk like that. Usually I just pretend I'm dumb. But that would never work here, and I wouldn't want to do it. I just about broke out in static electricity when she put her fingertips on my sleeve again.

"Where is that virtue I would claim with tense impersonal unworth, where does it dwell, that virtuous land where one can die without a second birth?"

I will admit it — I got scared by that sort of thing.

"Enough of death, now," I said. "Why would you go somewhere in search of such a thing? Now you have me asking questions! Let the critics die away. Let the poems come alive in your hands. People love your hands."

She took her fingers back and lifted the heavy glass with whisky in it. A cigarette appeared in her other hand. She smiled that funny little smile she does with her lips pursed.

"Peripatetics knew the value of posture: head up, head down?"

"Keep your head up, ma'am. Let that damned reviewer keep his head down another few decades."

"Poor cripple — knows the irrelevance of defeat?"

"It simply doesn't matter. He is long gone, and we are still here."

"And who are you and who am I?"

Ho ho. I felt a lot easier. Still loved her, too.

"I really don't know who I am, anymore. But you are our great lyric poet. You suggested that we were lovers, but you only indulge me, fair one."

"Dear, shall we move our hands together, or must we bear the onslaught of the tick, the tock, the icy draught of a clock's arms swinging themselves together — or now shall we kiss where once we laughed?"

She waved her glass back and forth now. It was empty. I did it again. To hell with the morning, I guess.

"I do not recall our laughing all that often," I said. "We live as long as we can, and we do not ask for happiness, do we? We ask for time to write our life. We ask every day for this time and this life."

"But who are we asking, and why do we ask?"

"I suppose that each person might have her own idea about that. Some people have God very much. Others have each other. I believe that you are blessed by a god I have never met. I do not know very much about gods. This god, female or male, has made you beautiful and good, and all those admirers I mentioned agree that you have passed the gift on."

"What are we whole or beautiful or good for but to be absolutely broken?"

"To exhibit grace, maybe."

"Insect, who are you?"

I sat up straight and looked scary. Like a big insect.

"I am the spirit of Armageddon past. I am he who hesitated, then turned and walked away from home and into mortality. That is why he needs poems, Spider Lady."

"Was it the donkey Death brayed out at him from the human mother's eyes, or did his love for her in that pause consume him?"

"It comes to the same thing, doesn't it? Each of us has to burn alone."

"What is there left for a faded star?"

"She needs only sleep. There will be plenty of fire tomorrow."

"Is she asleep now?"

"If she is asleep she is dreaming, and if she is dreaming, she is dreaming me, and if I am only a dream, how would I know how to advise you? Lord, I almost said 'thee!' No, the lady is awake. The fancy cannot cheat so well, and neither can yours truly."

II. Florence

I had been there before, but alone. She had been there years earlier, alone no matter what. Alone again, she referred to herself in the third person, a literary trick I was no stranger to. We were on the other side of the river, looking back and down at the gorgeous dusty-red city.

"Is the sun poring over her speech-wisdom, slipping hot money into her marvellous mouth?"

"It is an interesting suggestion," I allowed. "But no — I believe that her muse is nocturnal, missy. I see the moon caught in her horns."

I had learned just how to tease her, and I remain convinced that she liked it, my talent for it.

"But what should I care if her nightmares flourish?"

"They have, I propose, produced some of the best stanzas of our time and place."

"Where can we go?"

"I suggest that we stay here for a while. The day is warm. The palace persists through the centuries. We spent not a little effort to get here and up this hill."

She stepped slowly along the old path, and I saw that her clothes had been chosen so that a person with sufficient ignorance would see the Renaissance in her walking. I had plenty of ignorance.

"What is our reference?" she asked.

"Memory. I saw you stepping with your indelicate feet on flags you seemed to know."

"Why did we come with only our private recollection to a
garden on a quiet afternoon and Florence below explained
in persimmon sun?"

"Ha! I believe that this beauty and this care will answer
your question of last spring about a world full of hate and
broken things, milady. I will never forget the first time I
read your poem about this place."

"You strike me, Guardian, up there on your high wall, as
an archaic figure from the stiff past, or is it more the dusty
figures, tight and small, of my own childhood, my brothers', and our last flirtation with a land of make-believe
where toy soldiers doomed our zodiac?"

I took an obedient look in the direction of her somewhat
theatrical gaze.

"It is only the usual decoration indulged in by public art-
ists during the *quattrocento* or whenever," I suggested.

But she was into one of her *addresses*.

"Or am I wrong and you, with your straight back, are
indeed a true soldier of State, an aim-to-fire, shoot-to-kill
sort of guy, who'll look the bomb-packing Billy in his dyna-
mite eyes, pull your trigger first, then make your will?"

I put my arm around her Renaissance shoulders.

"If you are now addressing me rather than the patient guy
up there, I can tell you that I have never carried lance nor
sword nor blunderbuss nor Colt's .45. I am as peaceful and
devoid of weapon as you knew me in the sleeping car."

"Was it only last night?"

"I would hardly say 'only.' And I did not sleep at all for
the noise."

"Job's moaning, is it, the dark?"

"More like your moaning, I would say, when you found
out my peacefulness. Yet I have never wanted anyone so
much. Nor, if I have the secure sensitivity to judge, have I felt
someone's hospitality, if I may use that term, so keenly."

I suppose that all men, young or otherwise, are equally
insufferable in similar circumstances. I calmed down and
told her that I thought I'd perceived something she had
given.

"Maybe my body, maybe I?"

"Perhaps you two have differing dreams. Last night you called out the female version of my name. I felt that side of me wanting to respond, too."

"But when has my love ever been offered exactly and why should she be an exception?"

"I am not arguing that she should be; it is only a new sensation for me. I felt as though I had been born when the sun and the moon were both in the sky. I need educating again. I felt as though the moon were become my sun."

"If it is, tell me, who reads by that light?"

"I want only to be able to read you, at least a little."

"What are you sad about?"

"Sometimes, even when the page lies open, you are a closed book."

I had not noticed the moment when my arm left her shoulders.

"Why are you standing there staring?"

"I have come to Florence. It is summer. I see you standing before me. I stare at beauty, lady."

"What's that for?"

"Oh yes, I see, you only make it. You make it and make it, page after page. You never have to figure it out."

"What do you really want?"

All right.

"I want a total congress between your beauty and my mind. I want to know what is happening when you proffer an image I have never seen before. I want to know everything."

Now she put on her business face. She took out her long Italian cigarettes and her little gold ashtray with the lid. She sat on a *quattrocento* stone and crossed her legs.

"Are you talking about process and individuation. Or absolutes, whole numbers, that sort of thing?"

"Don't mock me. Whenever we start this kind of talk, I think we are going to discuss your work and its career among the good readers of our time. I had no idea that it would wend in this direction, no intention. I feel a little cornered, perhaps, forced to say things I want to keep from you and the world. Hah, world!"

"But why don't you do something?"

"I am abashed. Okay?"

"Why?"

"Well, because you are you. I am only this thing, me."

"Oh?"

"Yes. If I were able to use words easily I would tell you how it feels. As if the rainbow we saw yesterday were arched in my blood. It will quiver to life in my spirit, okay? You spoke of body. I feel as though my new, clean, naked body is rising to the light and the wind and the clean rain of heaven."

There was a silence. I didn't know whether this was because she found my language intemperate and ill-chosen. I would have been embarrassed if I weren't so uncharacteristically emotional, and away over here in Italy.

"Does it hurt?" she asked, and I could tell that she was trying to get me to look at her instead of the city. I did not have a really good idea what this was all about.

"Yes, damn it! I am burning," I said, trying not to be too loud. There were, after all, some tourists who had managed to make their way up this hill.

"Shall we call the fire engines?"

When I turned to look there was smoke coming out of her nostrils.

"I don't know whether you are making sport of me, or making images to be serious," I admitted.

"Will the little lady fall from her chair?"

"Don't call me that! You introduced me to her only last night. I have to get used to her. I never have an easy time with heavy new knowledge."

"Knowledge?"

I felt a sudden shift in my head, as if the Tuscan wine and sun had rushed across my brain. For the next few minutes I seemed to be talking in a dream. This was most unusual for me, at least in my adulthood. In the dream I spoke as well as I could, there in a doubly foreign country.

"Call it wisdom, then."

"Is there a shadow following the hand that writes always?"

I think that she was offering me a way down, into literary discussion again, where I might feel somewhat more safe.

"You are the one who wrote all those poems," I said, the tone of my voice letting her know how much I liked her, too. "They seem to have shadows enough for all."

"Or for the left-handed only?"

"Oh no, you will not introduce me to yet another side of myself! I have enough to cope with already, I would think. I cannot even figure out whether this is a vision or a waking dream."

III. In the Baltic

We were leaning on the rail while she smoked a long Swedish cigarette. Although it had still seemed to be summer to the south, the autumn was clearly here. Her high collar, dark purple and of some thick weave, rose as high as her crown of hair. Like many an ordinary traveller, she speculated about our fellow passengers.

"Shadow moves up the gang plank with us, is Chapter 7, 11, 13?"

"Oh no, the shadow!" I said, and I breathed salt air and tobacco smoke. "Okay, this shadow follows the writing hand even into the north. I suppose that if I can suffer all that noise in a Continental train, I can get used to a seaborne shadow. But I fear to know where this shade hails from." My language was getting dramatic again.

"If you can't recall the beginning and of time, who can get back there?"

So I quickly saw that my language was going to be pedestrian compared with hers. At times like this I liked to pretend that I could keep up. I squinted my eyes at the faint horizon.

"You are a demanding travel companion, lady. It will take

some getting used to, this third who sails with us," I said.

"Why is he so saintly, the reaches of his mind so vast and intimate?"

"I suppose he must be a sacrificed figure." I was really bluffing now. "I cannot believe we have got to this point in what I thought would be a pleasant tour with literary conversation. What did this fellow say to you while I gazed at the roof of the dome back there?"

" 'But what right had I to these highest joys?' "

"I suppose he was the anointed one. Why not just follow him, see where we are led? I will go with you anywhere, after all this."

IV. The Baltic Island

"Do we need a guide?" she asked in the morning of our third day there.

"What do you expect me to say?"

" 'What right have I to these highest joys?' "

"Oh, no. I am not the anointed one. Or rather, only in the sense that I have read those poems of yours that I keep trying to get the conversation back to. I follow. I want to be in your world."

Utter silence. We were the only ones at the cold beach, and there was not a gull and not a bit of wind for a gull to ride in. Finally she asked a question I was not expecting.

"Shall I tell you what I do to pass the time here on the island at night?"

"Of course. I will follow you to any part of your world." I was pretty familiar, I thought, with what she did at night.

"Russia, Suicide or France?"

"As long as I don't have to take up residency in any country I don't like."

"How do you ever find anything here?"

"Knowledge."

"Knowledge?"

"All right. The things we say or write without knowing them, without knowing what they are."

"Is there a shadow following the hand that writes always?"

I was not going to be led into that question about the shadow if I could help it. There were times when I was not certain whether we had said some things once before, or often . . .

"Not if the writer is like you, a queen in the darkness. Not if she has darkness in her veins. Knowledge of the kind you propose will never be knowledge for the likes of me, the simple, the nearly new-born. It is for others to write, for them who go out in the half-disastrous night, or who have it inside them."

I was pretty proud of that little speech. She dodged it.

"Or for the left-handed only?"

"Oh yes, you people. Whew! What is knowledge for you is only a shadow for us nearly new-born."

"Shadow moves up the with us is Chapter 7, 11, 13?"

I did not have a clue what she was saying, even if it was familiar. But I felt confident rather than lost for a change. Maybe my soul feels invigorated by a northern island.

"If that is the river, what is the boat, that's what I used to ask, when it was enough to appear vatic. Now I have been on that boat so long, I don't know where I am anymore, and as we are on a river, I don't know *when* I am, either."

"If you can't recall the beginning and of time, who can get back there?"

Confidence? What about bravado? I stood with my fists on my hips and looked out to the cold sea, a new Canute.

"Who cares, lady? It is enough for me to be here with you, wherever we are. Weren't we in some Italian town? Weren't you out all night with someone I was never introduced to? If I knew him I might measure him."

"Why is he so saintly, the reaches of his mind so vast and intimate?"

"I think he probably got as good as he took. What was the last thing he said to you?"

" 'But what right had I to these highest joys?' "

"He had none at all; it was nothing to do with rights. He should just have thanked his lucky fire folk in the sky. Let's go home."

"Do we need a guide?"

I put my coat-muffled arm around her coat-muffled waist and started walking us toward the inn.

"I wouldn't, after these past few nights, be surprised, milady," I said. "I have no idea what to say to you."

" 'What right have I to these highest joys?' "

"Touché." I bowed from my coat-muffled waist.

V. Off the B.C. Coast

"Shall I tell you what I do to pass the time here on the island at night?"

The gulls were squawking down in the harbour. The oolichans were probably swimming by the slippery pillars under the government wharf. The cormorants were spreading their wide wings to dry. We lay surrounded by books and carvings.

"All right. But this little room is an everywhere, babe. I can quickly imagine another home for you."

"Russia, Suicide or France?"

"I have been to all three of those places. I didn't see you there. Maybe we passed each other, like nights on the ship."

"How do you ever find anything here?"

"I open one of your books. I consider myself undeserving of what I find therein."

"Highest joys?"

"Sometimes. Among other, let us say, extremities."

"Or an oath?"

"If an oath is equivalent to inspired language, as important as the phrase whose source Valéry traced to heaven.

The inspired first, and as happens so often in these books, last words."

"Whoever died like that with such good manners?"

Every time her mind darted like that, I felt challenged to reply quickly, but I preferred to make my way carefully. I would usually try to fill the slight time by kissing her knuckles or fixing a strand of hair behind her ear.

"Good manners? I have wondered whether that is your secret for staying alive despite all the foreboding words. ..."

"Such elegance of speech and intricacy of thought?"

"Such music, milady. The food I avail myself of when I cannot feed alone."

"Will you remember to pay the debt?"

"You mean by trying to form my own hobbled verses? Dragged down by human, mortal thought? What did your shadow under the dome tell you about that enterprise?"

" 'For is not philosophy the study of death?' "

"As for me, my former friends tell me that they are tired of that subject in my poor works."

" '*Pourquoi es-tu si triste ma chère?*' "

I did not know whom she was quoting. I knew it wasn't her famous shadow.

"I am mortal," I said.

" '*Pourquoi es-tu si triste?*' "

"I don't have any news from the abode where the immortals are. All right?"

" '*Pourquoi es-tu si triste, chérie?*' "

"I am aware that you are quoting, you torturer. I just don't know wherefrom."

She removed my light fingers from her and gave me a good long purple stare.

"Am I responding to your books or you?" she asked at last.

"Don't read my books," I said, probably with a measure of petulance, if the truth be told. "Read someone useful. Read some great Canadian thinker from back east."

" 'Where is here?' "

"Exactly."

"Whatever happened to The News of the World?"

"If it was half-decent poetry it is still around," I said.

"After survival, what?"

"Well, I suppose it becomes, I don't know, runic."

"The sedition in my own hand, will it be written down legibly, will I sign it and hand it over for someone else to fulfill?"

"That's the idea." At the time, I thought I followed what she was saying. Later I wasn't so sure.

"Or will I open like a Venus fly-trap to catch fat spies from the enemy lines and feed myself forever on them on them on them?"

I sort of laughed, sort of snorted.

"They are not worth the candle. They are as far behind you as that poor reviewer we were talking about talking about talking about."

"I shaft my needle again and again into hell's veins and heaven's, listening for messages pulsing on whose bloody hopes?"

"They can't be mine. You know that I have never been to those places."

I never liked it when the talk got around to hell and heaven. Not that those places scared me. Just that she scared me when she talked about them. She could have been a priest refusing to shrive herself.

"Whose love, tell me, o love's divine airs, elaborates the oratorio?"

"We've been to Florence. I'll guess Dante's."

"Who loved him before his marriage at age thirty-six?"

"I am a poor scholar. I didn't even know he was married. Was he running around on his wife when he went chasing after Beatrice?"

She was not listening to me, not interested in listening. She was not lying beside me, either, but lifting the lid of a square tin tea box and peeking inside.

"Who did he lust for or sleep with, and who shifted his

decorous sweetness into plain-song, pain-song, body to body?"

I swung my feet to the floor. I could hear a small seaplane buzzing the harbour.

"I always thought his song was a long way from plain. But I understand that he was quite a departure for his time, writing in some regional Italiano instead of Latin. I suppose the Church fathers objected that they had to speak Latin, God's language, in those three worlds he claimed to have visited."

"Three?"

"Hell, Purgatory and Paradise. Or as you lately put it, Russia, Suicide and France. I have not been within a country mile of any of them."

"Mile?"

"I have not been within a canto of any of them. No man is an — "

"Island?"

" — immortal."

VI. The Okanagan Valley

We were sitting in my Toyota, halfway up a brown mountain, looking at twenty kilometers of the valley, green fruit trees, invisible river. We were looking through a sheaf of white and coloured papers.

"Why, how, oh God, has it come to this — "

"Come on, lady. I have never seen so much mortality in poetry as I have seen in yours. We live surrounded by the edges of death."

" — hook, sickle, scythe to cut us down this mark?"

"Well, yes, if you are going to go agricultural in your tropes. Come on, cheer up! Look at the beautiful mortal landscape we get to play our little parts in. Delicious fruit hangs from the trees, urging us to pluck."

"Who — how many years to shape the mind to make its turn toward this?"

"Mind is shapely. Its subject is its own desire for immortality, carried as it is inside vegetation that will ripen and fall. Read the writing on the wall."

I know where that tired trope came from. The high school graduates had decorated the stone cliffs behind us with their first names. An odd ambition.

"The where/when of the type, the proper fall of lead in the printer's font?"

"There you go! We're all going to become fertilizer. While we are here we can make lovely books that will outlive us, but probably not Dante."

"And who are you in this school room torture chamber, whose are you?"

"I am your rapt pupil," I said, a little smugly. "Here in this classroom, which some people might call a verdant valley, I am your humble student. I am to you as you are to Dante."

"And what of your trials and errors?"

"All emanate from my heart, Miss."

"Does it know what I say?"

"Ah, I read your verses to it every night."

"Can it imagine my sentence?"

"If I keep quiet and give it space to dream."

"Where did your mouth go?"

I took a look over at her. She was not smiling. She was not gazing out at the panorama. She was looking straight at me.

"I kept it shut, Ma'am."

"Why didn't you say hello?"

"I had never been away from you. In my heart you were ever there. You seemed to live there. My heart has chambers where my lady may be, half of that couple in an everywhere."

" 'And Hollywood?' "

"I never added that phrase."

" 'Hollywood next?' "

"If you insist. But your glamour seems to me a greater

sort. Unless you say Hollywood as a metonym. As a sign perhaps, only."

There was, though I had not seen any female scrabbling in tilted slightly raised handbag, a cigarette in her mouth. I pushed the lighter in.

"Who knows?" She was not pretending the melancholy I heard.

"Not I," was all I could say.

"Who knows?"

"Not even Dante. Not the father of us all."

"Why not the sun?"

"What did the sun ever do for you, Dark Lady. What did the sun ever say to you?"

" 'Where is the *Duende*?' "

"You cannot make *Duende* while the sun shines. The *Duende* stepped long ago into the shadow. She frightens the cattle as she passes."

I was talking fancy again. Sometimes I liked that; sometimes I was embarrassed, or maybe browned off at myself. The lighter popped out. I lit her cigarette, and she sort of noticed.

"What was the path she took?"

"The *Duende*? A circumlocutory one, for certain. A circumlunary one, mayhap."

"As winding as her gut with the pain in it?"

"Now that's funny. I never thought of the *Duende* herself suffering. *Duende* means soft, doesn't it? No? In Mexico City I once used a toilet paper called "*Duende*." That was a joke, I remember. So now this *Duende* of yours wanders with pain."

"Along the beach?"

"In all likelihood, under the beach moon."

"To the caves in the hill?"

"Ah, caves make us think of poetry. Well, this valley is full of beaches and caves. We are so careful, aren't we, to choose an apt place to conduct our business."

"Did Wilson ever think of that before he shot himself so tidily in his office?"

I did not like this kind of turn in her talk. In her questions. I was used to them, but I could never get comfortable with them. I started the car and backed away from the dry cliff. Then I turned, and headed back toward the surfaced road, that snake of old pavement in the hills. I was watching to make sure that she put the cigarette in the ashtray. When we reached the pavement I replied to her Wilson question.

"Wilson did not believe in spooks, much less the Good Witch Poesy. He was a scientist. Shelley might have read all the latest science, but he was a poet."

"So what if Lowry got spooked by sea-birds and volcanoes crossing?"

Boy, all these writers, all these men on beaches.

"I guess you could say that for his own reasons he could not cleave the apparent from the real, eh?" I was hoping that she would catch the reference, and that it would lighten things. I should have known better. The orchards moved past our side windows.

"Who can survive that mad illumination shining in eyes, pouring over the stone?" She sat perfectly still, not smoking, not fingering the mist on the window, not, one could be sure, reaching toward me.

"Well, you have, so far," I said. "I like to think that I will be able to. That we, for instance, will."

"Shall you or I smash out that multiple illumination?"

"Whew! That's hard to say: mul-ti-pull-ill-umin-ation."

"Did I say illumination?"

"More than once, Babe."

"Illumination, twin beat of flinty wings, one-eyed illumination?"

"Sounds like that train we were on last spring."

"Can I really say I found even two cents at the crossing?"

"We didn't even slow down at any crossings."

"Am I the one with wings fixed on with faulty glue?"

"We all are. Even Dante was, I'll wager. We all feel that way, even while readers are singing praises. Well, you know more about praises than I do. Young poets are saying your name all the time now."

We were at the motel next to the little drab airport. On our side of the fence there was a swimming pool with small locust trees around it. On the other side there was a narrow old paved landing strip and a lot of crisp tumbleweed. I helped her out of the car, and we went straight to our room. It was a peculiar room, in a corner tower, round, with lots of windows, lots of window curtains.

"Or am I the angelic form doting, unfaithful, and true?"

She unwound her mauve scarf and I took it from her.

"I would gladly accept any of those from you," I told her. "In Russia, Purgatory or France."

"Is this what Auden knew, that the pair are secretly bored, cruising that River of Light, scaring the illiterate horde?"

"I am never bored in your company. Milady. I am not Dante and you are no teenaged beauty. But while I don't expect to glimpse you in Paradise any time soon, I would never yawn in your presence. We have been around for a while, but — "

"Too old to mate, do they get from Alighieri's shore a voyeuristic view of this small round polished floor which makes us passionate, or leaves us cold — and late?"

"Too old? What about last — "

"Who is this woman I know only slightly?"

Another quick turn. Now her eyes were only centimetres from me, and they were looking hard into mine.

"I told you, you introduced her to me one night in a sleeping car. I've been carrying her around inside me for years, but never met her before. I am not at all comfortable talking about her," I whispered.

"What was, I am asking, antecedent to the critical delirium of love that did not give birth?"

Her mouth was at my ear. Valley light came in windows

at every side, and bounced off mirrors. Quickly, I tried to recall what had been antecedent.

"Well, a pretty decent meal, given the standards of railroad fare. Then some pretty inflammatory conversation, principally from your corner, as I recall."

"Why what I am asking I pushed out was only the idiot addition of one and one make two?"

"Sometimes I can't make head nor tail of your syntax, my lovely and now shoeless friend. But on the occasion that I believed we were referring to, your questions were just the opposite in kind: straight and repetitive. You kept asking when the caribou would come. I said I was no caribou. You were no caribou horsewoman."

"Why was it we who were magic animals could not fit into poems and be happy?"

"All animals, someone said hundreds of years ago, are sad after you know what."

I had hung the scarf up carefully. Now I was adding to it.

"What was, I am asking, required of us beyond cages we carried in case?"

"I stepped willingly into your cage long ago. I require nothing of you. I eagerly supply anything that is required of me. I told you that four years ago, after the reading."

"Love four years, only hyperventilating four fears, I owe you for what?"

"Whatever the hell that means. Here, lift your arm a second. You said I had brought you the pearl of great price. I said it was free, remember? Surely you kept it all these years, separated as we have been so often."

"In shell's pink growing, birth of the world, feathery flesh or love what matter?"

"What matter. Well. Another woman told me that she would gladly lose her kingdom for it."

"It?"

"At least you were polite enough not to remind me that pearls are the result of irritation. I also hope that they have been at least a source of some irritation for you, cruel woman."

"They?"

"Oh, I suppose they were all one to you. You do sometimes seem to live in the present rather than memory. But one can also love the things one remembers."

Now she smiled at last, and the sunshine bathed her skin from all sides. She was not exactly looking at me, though.

"Remember Maureen, the Trout Quintet, that summer of '51 in Montreal?" she said.

"I did not get to Montreal until 1954, and then I was an ignorant boy. The only poem I had read was a translated Omar Khayyam. Lord!"

"Who dances in Persia Now?"

"You can get into trouble for dancing in Persia. It is Iran now. Oh, I think that when a nation stops being great or interesting, it should be erased from memory. Tossed into the trash and emptied."

"What should I tell her who can see in the mirror the chance of a bird standing on one pink leg?"

I liked it when she asked one like that. I always liked to imagine that it was quick invention, nothing to do with immediate data.

"If she is in Iran," I said, "tell her to close all the doors and windows and pull the cloth tight under her eyes. Tell her there will be a poet in Persia again in another five hundred years."

"Tell her to shut her eyes tight, boil her ears in essence of camellias, turn herself over to the green haunt orchid on the next blue Monday?"

"Tell her whatever you want. I renounce all hope or interest."

"Why should I tell her anything?"

"One: you are a poet. You cannot help yourself. Two: your name is on the lips of all the young women who have considered art or death. Or a decent line of anything. If they haven't heard of you in Iran, well, they should."

Now the valley sun was suddenly gone, behind a bare mountain that looked like a 1947 Pontiac.

"Grey-eyed dryad," she said, "have you seen one, if only for the sound of grey-eyed dryad?"

"If you are alluding to the poet I think you are alluding to, you could not lead an acolyte to a path more true. That or a pestle with a pistil."

"What do you mean in this religious dark damning me with feathers and your hot light?"

"I was not even quite making fun of you, oh sensitive soul. We were talking about memory, I think. Surely you can remember something worth loving, some line of something?"

"What 'passed seven times,' and what 'shall be for a time, and times, and a half'?"

"Now I'm afraid I have no idea whom you are quoting. It doesn't quite sound like that dryad you mentioned. This confabulation is getting a little *outré*. I am lost in the forest, if you want to put it in poetic terms. Is that where dryads live? Forests?"

"Mulberry tree with innocent eyes, Catalpa with your huge hands, I am looking at you, so why can't you look back?"

"Oh boy. Come into the deep woods, my lady. Find what awaits you, if you're not chicken."

I won't tell you what I was doing while I said this, but I would not expect you to in my place, either.

"Or should I save myself with long voyages?"

"Jesus, we are *on* a long voyage!" I said, not shouting, just saying it vigorously. "If you are worried about saving your soul, you should not have come here in the first place."

"My soul, my soul, who said that?"

"What the hell else have you got to save? Oh, I shouldn't have said that. Sorry. Still — "

"What shall we do tonight?"

"What we did last night would be fine with
about what we did last night?"

"Tonight, tonight, love, what shall we do tonight?"

"All right. I get it. How about if we just stay here in the
god damned woods?" Bitter irony, native land. Desert of my
heart, my valley. When Creeley talked about his childhood
woods, I had to imagine, trees close *together.*

"Is there such a thing as a vulgar plant?"

"You called me an insect earlier in the year. Thanks for
the promotion."

"Will the haiku butterfly decorously settle on the bronze
bell?"

"I'm not in a haiku mood. I feel more like a big violent
scene in an epic. I feel like sounding off with a catalogue
of all the horses and weapons and great warriors, and then
starting up the god damned clashing and gutting."

"Whose song is this anyway?" she asked, blowing sweet
smoke past my ear.

"It's still a song? Okay, okay. Sorry I got a little animated
there. Yes, it is still your song. Yes, you are still the singer
the young ones want to hear."

"Is it a song being sung on the narrow road to the
North?"

"It, and we, will go wherever you list. If we find that you
have made another book, we will see that as a bonus. You
could call it, if you list, *The Narrow Road to the North.* You
can call it *Where the Hell are the Caribou?* What would
you like to call it?"

"*Why Poetry?*"

"You won't call it that."

"And why not?"

"Because it does not suggest any thinking about the subject, of course. Oh, hell, I just remembered what you have
always said about that."

" 'Why don't you speak of feelings?' "

"Exactly. Well, it is not that I don't have feelings, which I

now. It is just that when I am overcome
nnot be trusted to write poems. I go to
t, for thinking. I even go to *your* poems

most *peculiar* glance. I pulled all the

ne. How   143

VII. At Karnak, briefly

"And when you die at the executioner's hands do you also
quote poems, Amin?"

I had wrapped myself in a sheet. My mustache bristled.

"I doubt it greatly," I said with a desert accent.

"Why not?"

"Do you know how many times I have been in the executioner's hands? I mean if we are forced to talk poetry
here? When you are in the executioner's hands, you do not
think of verses. All you can think of is disappearance. You
want to disappear from the executioner's gaze; otherwise
he will be in charge of your disappearance. Oh, I know you,
Missy. You are going to tell me that poetry is the art of
disappearance."

I twirled. My hem went way out there.

"Oh You who keep disappearing behind a black cloud like
a woman behind her veil, how do you feel, shut off like that
from the perfect obedience of your worshippers?"

"I have news for you, babe. I don't have worshipper one.
The young say your name nearly all the time now. They
are writing dissertations on your skin. But they have not
heard of me, even after I am made, on some rare occasion,
required reading. It's you they have up there between them
and the firmament."

"The slouch of the ground, do you hear that?"

"Oh, I do. Indeed I do. I've never left it."

"Why should we ever come down, ever?"

"There are times when you don't. When you do, I don't
find your flesh too too solid at all."

"Remember Asad, Ghalib?"

I got the message that she was playing a part. I was supposed to play a part, too. I looked at a stone pillar with a lily carved on its top.

"I don't know the gentlemen," I said. "I take it that they have something to do with that ancient middle eastern stuff you have been reading and, uh, writing. And, by the way, I have never before answered to the name Amin."

"Mirza Asadullah Beg Khan, who are you really?"

I looked at a lily. I saw the line of cobras along a wall.

"None of the above. You had it right last night on the train. That nasty word."

"Sir?"

She was coy. She was brazen. She was a pharaoh's wife and a god's daughter.

"Oh, when we made that little compartment an everywhere. And now I have been everywhere, man."

"My face?"

"Included. I think you've been a lot of places, too. They don't have to be in silken Ptolemaic climes, and they don't have to be in days of yore. You've been a lot of places where I had a good look at you."

"On bended knee?"

"Yep, and that was no proposal, fair damosel."

She looked me full in the face, and I could have counted to twenty. Then she walked on the dust between pillars, perhaps reading the writing on the wall. When in the company of gods, she loved and was loved, no doubt about that. The first time I had ever seen her I thought of Cleopatra, and I know that most men did. I was not at all suicidal, and I had no ancestors that were immortal. I walked fast enough to catch up to her. I leaned my face into her vision. I wanted her to read me as if I were a cartouche.

"Why this obsession?" she asked, a little tired tenderness creeping into her imperial voice. It was like moonlight on the Nile. Or so I expected. We had not been there at night yet.

"It ain't an obsession," I whispered. "It is the dearest old-time subject of our art."

"The Romance of Revolution?"

"If need be. A ditty of no tone. The agony of the feet."

"The last agony of the Oedipus complex?"

"The first verses of the Herpes simplex."

"The anxiety of (patriarchal) influence?" Now she was as light as I had heard her for a month. She was looking forward, I knew, to a visit from Thoth.

"That ain't poetry at all," I said, the tone of my voice encouraging lightness. "That is the stuff graduate students have to memorize. That is the post-Marxist circus."

What, I thought, a strange place to be talking about *that*.

VIII. Approaching St. Petersburg

"Did it look very different in April, 1917?"

"Well, there were a lot more communists around," I said.

"Will the *Intourist* greeter be there at the station?"

I laughed. Then I leaned toward her seat and touched the dark plum cloth on her forearm.

"Are you kidding? By the time we get there we will be familiar figures for a good medium-sized bureaucracy. I hope that she is a tall blonde with a sad beauty like the first winter wind across the Neva. That's what I got last time in St. Petersburg."

"Was it a prophetic vision of the tourism industry?"

"Seemed more like a woman in good stockings, worried that she might get an idiom wrong. She had a well-drilled civic and national pride."

"Or the deep down *conservateur* instinct?"

"Probably. Does that make her a poet's friend? Equal? She was shy but nearly bursting with a sense of the importance of her job."

"Post-war delusions of grandeur, or make-work?" She was

turned almost completely around now, to look out the window at the low yellow buildings along the creeping river.

"No more of either than we with our rimes carry around. I figure that if it is not a tie, the score is pretty close."

"610–546?"

"Something like that," I said.

The train was going really slowly now. We were almost *there*. It is truly exciting to arrive at such a place in such a time.

"Which way is blowing?" she asked, her eyes staring sharp into mine, looking through those big eyeglasses, an old-time socialist in a train.

"Which way is *what* blowing?" I had never heard her talk that way.

"Is blowing the lid off your head?"

"Only thing does that is a great ethnic joke or a — "

"Poem?"

"Huh? Well, yours often do the trick, milady. When I open one of your books (and as you know, I take them with me when I travel like this), I am encouraged to see that there is at least one poet doing what a poet should be doing."

We were under the arcing roof of the station now, but she was looking straight into my eyes, as if we were at her kitchen table on the hill among the trees on a Gulf island. I thought that she would be looking for statues of Lenin, looking for scenes from a black Eisenstein film. No.

"And there are the poets doing what?"

"Jacking around," I said in my agitation. "Reading theory. Telling the stories of their lives. Knocking off anecdotes. I know one old poet who still thinks he is a shock to the system."

"What does he want?"

"Personal immortality and prompt payment by his renters, I think."

Now she knew whom I meant. A one-time socialist. Still she teased me.

"Contributions to knowledge?"

"He thinks that all knowledge has been attained, and that he has a grip on the sum."

"Civilization and its discontents?"

"He claims to be Nietzsche's truest follower. We, on the other hand, are going where we are going to find something unsettled and probably unsettling. You agree?"

"Chaos among the order — or, oh yes, french doors opening onto a deck and a small pool where we can watch our weird reflections shimmering and insubstantial?"

I could not believe this, but I was enjoying it. It was kind of *glamorous*, talking this way while we watched our suitcases being put into a minibus on the side of the prospect in this most peculiarly unfamiliar city, climbing into the vehicle and heading god knows where, to a hotel with gold-leaf, probably. She just kept on talking this way, firing the questions. I think she noticed every nuance of post-revolutionary street life.

"Unsubstantial is the key word," I said, nevertheless changing it slightly. "You got it. This writing stuff is not what another old gink I know of claims it is, a kind of clever protection of the language. It's a little more chancy than that. What, for instance, is your main concern, mid-writing?"

"How to get out of the poem without a scratch?"

"Right." I was passing U.S. dollar bills to everyone who had a hand. Now at last we were in our room, and the window was old enough that it would open. There was a camera store with Japanese names written in the neonized Cyrillic alphabet in its window. "And from what I have heard, that doesn't happen very often. That's happened to me a few times. Do you remember what you asked yourself the last time you survived a poem? Or remember the way I looked when you came over and found me on my couch with that broken pen in my hand?"

"As you lay there dying in seizure was it your lord Life or your lord Death who came to collect a last poem as you careened into the *beautiful darkness?*"

"At the time I would not have been able to distinguish one from the other. I just followed the figure who appeared, followed where he went."

I joined her on the tsar-sized bed and we lay side by side on our backs, resting in northeast Europe.

"And was it really beautiful?" she persisted.

"How the hell should I know? I was mostly dead. I could hardly see out of my red eyes."

"Was it dark?"

"Dark as your soul, you might say. I think I threw my pages behind me as we disappeared."

"Or did the cat get your last fabulous word?"

"I keep my cats out in the yard," I reminded her. "Your cats, on the other hand, are capable of walking through walls, from what I have heard. They have wide frenzied eyes after what they have seen."

We had not turned on the room's lights, if there were any. Outside we could see a cobalt sky above the low yellow prospect, and it was becoming dark in the room. I left the window open, though the air that came in along with motorcycle noise was not warm.

"The romantic couple cast long glances and smoke from their silver lair; birds zoom down like missiles, testing testing?"

All I knew was that she was indulging her fancy for invention. Sometimes it worked better than at other times. I just kept on about cats.

"Oh, my cats wouldn't even notice. Yours, on the other hand — "

"Have I struck the right note?"

"I think so. Here, let me open one of your books." I dug into my haversack and pulled out the one with pale rocks on the cover. "Have a look."

She flipped through, tilting the page to catch a faint light. She sat up on the side of the bed.

"Who is this *I* infesting my poems?"

I sat up too, and put my left arm around her shoulders. I

took the book from her elegant fingers with the very big rings.

"Ho ho. That is the subject of half the essays all your critics and acolytes fill special issues of respected magazines with. They think they may be able to tell the apparent from the real."

I snorted. She imitated my snort. Now *that* was both funny and a little embarrassing for *some* reason.

"Is it I hiding behind the Trump type on the page of the book you are reading?"

I closed the book quickly. I didn't even keep a thumb inside.

"My friend of longest duration is named Trump," I said. "I don't even know where *he* is most of the time? How would I know where *you* are to be found? I go to your books looking for you, but if I have any brain left, I don't expect to shake hands with you in the middle of some dark continent. Or the edge."

"Is it a photograph of me on the cover of *Wilson's Bowl?*"

I didn't tell her that I had often wondered the same thing. I had an argument to make now.

"Do you mean on the back cover flap or the front cover flap? Even your questions are full of questions. About one of them, people will say 'Oh, that's you,' and about the other one, they will say 'That looks like you,' or 'That could be you.' Vasereli is a red telephone booth. Anything is possible. Hell, when you are not asking questions you are reporting on the questions you asked someone else. Those old ginks I mentioned at least live in a self-made world constructed out of answers. I might not know what is happening when I read your poems, but I *hear* them. Someone is speaking. I find *someone* there."

"Is it I?" Big smile.

"Oh, Christ!"

"Or am I reading, as they say, 'in person', in the first person?"

"Leave me alone. I can't — "

"*Listen:* Do you hear the *I* running away with the man in the green hat?"

I was not going to let her beat me at this one on a darkening evening in old Saint Pete. I liked it that she was teasing me. I wished that she would do that more often, frankly. But what could I do? I was not going to let her have the last word, question or not.

"I got *him* spotted," I said, standing up and straightening my clothes. "He's either your Lord Life or your Lord Death, or maybe he's Yours Truly. This is a very romantic trip we have been taking, Doll. This I you are talking about? I travelled with her because she is so mysterious. I saw her from a distance, bending to pick something up. How could I not rush to her side to help?"

Imagine! I called her *Doll!*

"But what did she lift: toothbrush, tampax, iron pills, flea collar, vaginal spray, videotapes, alarm clock, perfume, shampoo, peroxide, garbage bags?"

I shrugged there in the dark. Her eyeglasses caught a glint of light from the window and reminded me that she was wearing them, as Catherine never had, at least in public.

"Okay, sure, all of the above," I conceded. "If you are going to call your first-person person 'she,' I am going to call her happy momentary consort 'he.' He loves her *apparent* as much as he adores her *real*. I think that he admitted to that feeling (remember feelings?) in the train again last night."

"What does he think?" asked her voice from the dark. I heard her glasses on the glass top of the bedside table. I felt a thrill across my belly.

"It all emanates from his heart. It all appears before us as a beautiful mortal landscape we get to play our little parts in. And in Baskerville type, by the way," I said.

"Intaglio for what you see best, the 'empty imprint'?"

"Wilson's bowl is intaglio, isn't it?" I asked, stepping toward the dark. "That's what that figure you call 'she' is walking away from on the inside flap of the front cover."

Someone's voice came out of the dark. It seemed to wrap around my head. I was having a witty conversation about a poetry book written on the eastern edge of another ocean?

"What does she think as she sits on the verge, this side of anonymous water?" asked the voice.

"She is not sitting, dear. You are standing. A solitary delicate beast. Standing. Past the place where it can hear them all speaking her name."

I did not know what I was saying, but from the way her hands moved now, I knew that she had me figured out perfectly.

☐ The Home for Heroes

A Parable

It was a large room, almost bare. High on one wall was a bell-shaped loudspeaker. There was a high wooden stool, the kind that folksingers used to sit on, right in the middle of the room. On the wall opposite the loudspeaker there was a boxer's speed punching bag. There were no drapes, no paintings, no hangings of any kind. Well, there was a blackboard on the back wall. It was about a metre and a half wide. There were no windows, but there was a door. Only one door, so naturally it could be opened, as far as anyone knew.

That's as much as Mr. Aligari knew anyway. He was a short man dressed in a business suit and fashionable eyeglasses. As we look in on the scene he appears to be sitting on the floor, or perhaps more as if he were half-sitting, half-fallen. His hat, one of those green affairs that look as if they have been influenced by an advertisement for Alpine Holiday fun, lies on the floor beside him. Yes, he appears to have fallen there, though from no great height. He seems to be just regaining enough consciousness to be able to look around and see where he is. In no way is he injured.

He gets shakily to his feet and looks around him, apparently puzzled to find himself in such a place. He picks up his hat and holds it in one hand while he walks around the room, finally coming to the door. He tries the door and finds it locked. As he turns his back on it, it silently opens, stays part way open for a moment, then just as silently closes. Mr. Aligari walks around the room again, touches the stool, touches his finger to the blackboard, looks at the punching bag. He prepares to take a swing at the punching bag, but stops himself. He walks to the blackboard and picks a piece of thick chalk from the sill, prepares to write on the blackboard, then stops himself.

He walks to the door and tries it again, but it is locked. He goes to the blackboard and prepares to write, but stops himself again. Then he reaches up and letters in big blocks: WHERE AM I?

He walks around the room again, this time feeling for secret doors. Then he comes back to the blackboard, hesitates, picks up a blackboard eraser from the sill and wipes out the words. He letters in blocks: WHEN AM I?

LOUDSPEAKER: The time is exactly 4:30.

MR. ALIGARI: I have to get up at 6:30. [*Pause*] I'll be no good at work in the morning.

LOUDSPEAKER: The time is exactly 9:00 p.m.

MR. ALIGARI: [*Looking up at loudspeaker*] See if you can do any better with my other question.

There's a silence for a long fifteen seconds. Then the door opens and a man enters. He is athletic, dressed in a comic-strip superhero uniform, complete with cape and so on. This person closes the door behind him, then walks over to the blackboard, and with immaculate care, erases the lettering. He then goes to the stool and sits atop it, careful with his cape. Only then does he look at Mr. Aligari.

THE MAN OF STEEL: You in sports?

MR. ALIGARI: [*moving toward the door*] Weekend golf. A little water skiing.

THE MAN OF STEEL: Comics?

MR. ALIGARI: [*at the door*] What?

THE MAN OF STEEL: You in a comic strip?

MR. ALIGARI: Not up till now, no.

Mr. Aligari tries the door. It is still locked. There is no reaction on the part of The Man of Steel.

THE MAN OF STEEL: War?

MR. ALIGARI: No.

· THE MAN OF STEEL: Books? Movies? Exploring? Wrestling?

MR. ALIGARI: [*with some impatience*] No.

THE MAN OF STEEL: Well, what are you in?

MR. ALIGARI: That is precisely what I would like to know.

THE MAN OF STEEL: Aren't you a hero?

MR. ALIGARI: What the hell are you talking about? I'm just a junior executive of a confectionery organization. I'm also a commuter. I'm a husband and a father, sort of. During the war I was a conscientious objector. Once I was a waiter on the railway. I have varicose veins, anyway. Not a hero. No. Not hero material. [*He sounds a tad sarcastic.*] Not the stuff heroes are made of. Right now I'm probably either late at home or late at the shop. The office. I can't seem to find out where I'm supposed to be because I don't know whether it's morning or night.

THE MAN OF STEEL: Hell, I've got varicose veins. In my legs. In my neck. I've got a boil, too. And I get short of breath from flying.

MR. ALIGARI: I'm disillusioned. Or I would be if I could concentrate on it.

THE MAN OF STEEL: You're not a hero, eh?

MR. ALIGARI: I'm a flop, actually. I can't even sell candies, or so Didi says. My wife. [*He adds as a confidential explanation:*] I'm a daydreamer, according to her.

THE MAN OF STEEL: Well, what are you doing here?

MR. ALIGARI: I don't have the slightest idea. Why don't you ask him? [*He gestures toward the loudspeaker.*]

LOUDSPEAKER: The time is exactly 12:15.

As if that were a signal, The Man of Steel gets off the stool, goes to the blackboard, and letters in large blocks: THE MAN OF STEEL.
  Aligari now sits on the stool, puts his hat on his head, and watches distractedly.

LOUDSPEAKER: Look! Up in the sky! It's a bird!

THE MAN OF STEEL: Ah, I know now. [*Addressing Mr. Aligari*] You're still in your secret identity.

MR. ALIGARI: I'll say!

LOUDSPEAKER: Faster than a speeding pullet!

The Man of Steel runs slowly and in a stumbling gait around the room, a look of haggard desperate pride in his face.

LOUDSPEAKER: The Man of Steel!

The Man of Steel swings mightily at the punching bag, misses completely, and sprawls on the floor.

MR. ALIGARI: [*To the loudspeaker*] Leave him alone!

THE MAN OF STEEL: Isn't anyone going to help me up?

Mr. Aligari goes over and helps The Man of Steel to his feet, then walks away from him in disgust.

THE MAN OF STEEL: Well, how would *you* like it? I'd sell my soul not to be a hero, believe you me. The first chance I got, so help me —

Stuck for a word or name, he stops. He walks hurriedly to the blackboard and wipes it clean. Then he leaves the room in a hangdog manner.

   Mr. Aligari once more tries the door, and once more finds it locked. He gets his cigarettes out and tries to light one. The first three matches do not ignite the cigarette. After the first failed match he looks around for an ashtray, and finally drops the dead match into his jacket pocket. Puzzled, he wets a forefinger and lifts it into the air. There is, of course, no breeze. He shrugs his shoulders, and gets set to try a fourth match.

LOUDSPEAKER: No smoking! Thank you for not smoking.

Mr. Aligari puts the cigarette back into its package and puts the package and his matches away.

LOUDSPEAKER: You may smoke if you like.

Mr. Aligari does not bother smoking. He has his back to the door and his head down as another man enters and sits on the stool. This is a robust man in a baseball uniform, complete except for team insignia. He carries a heavy baseball bat. He walks to the blackboard and letters in big blocks: THE SULTAN OF SWAT. Then he takes a perch on the stool.

THE SULTAN OF SWAT: [*Diffidently*] Want an autograph?

MR. ALIGARI: [*Looks up at the newcomer.*] You too? What are you doing here? What did you ever do to be here?

THE SULTAN OF SWAT: [*Peers at Mr. Aligari as if interrogating him.*] You think you have to do some-thing to get sent here?

MR. ALIGARI: I am just trying to figure out where and when [*snaps his head to look at the loudspeaker*] I am. You must have done something.

THE SULTAN OF SWAT: Drove in a lot of runs.

MR. ALIGARI: Must have done something, to wind up with a stool and a blackboard.

THE SULTAN OF SWAT: And a punching bag and a —

MR. ALIGARI: What did you do?

THE SULTAN OF SWAT: I?

MR. ALIGARI: You. Both of you. All of you, I'm guessing.

THE SULTAN OF SWAT: Well, why not? Didn't you ever get a stomach ache from eating a lot of some-thing you really like? And you can't help it. You never think of the stomach ache till you have it. Every time.

MR. ALIGARI: Mmm. Well, I for one do not deserve a stomach ache or any kind of ache. I shouldn't be here at all. Someone has obviously made a mistake.

THE SULTAN OF SWAT: I think I've heard that before.

MR. ALIGARI: As for you, I can't say. I figure you belong here.

THE SULTAN OF SWAT: I can't do a thing right since I got traded into this league.

MR. ALIGARI: Well, tomorrow is another day.

THE SULTAN OF SWAT: Don't say that!

The Sultan of Swat goes into a fit of violent laughter that makes Mr. Aligari step backward. The Sultan of Swat swings his bat around his head. Still laughing, he swings it at the punching bag and misses. Immediately, his laughter stops and he stands still, his back to the audience, the bat drooping from his loose arm.

LOUDSPEAKER: The time is Tuesday, October 4th.

The Sultan of Swat immediately goes to the blackboard and wipes it clean. He goes to the door with his bat dragging behind him.

THE SULTAN OF SWAT: [*Going out the door*] Ever had your picture in the paper? [*He goes out, closing the door behind him.*]

MR. ALIGARI: In the company newsletter oncc, a group picture of the bowling team.

LOUDSPEAKER: Have your return route ticket stubs ready, please.

Mr. Aligari takes a handful of paper money and other paper out of his pocket, finds his ticket stub, and holds it ready.

LOUDSPEAKER: Attention! All flights have been cancelled.

A third hero enters the room. He is large and husky, and has a fan-shaped white beard of medium length. He wears aviator glasses with steel rims. He is dressed as if for a safari — shorts, puttees, boots, shirt, hunting vest, peaked cap, all in khaki. He is carrying a high-powered rifle with a scope sight and sling over his shoulder, a portable typewriter without a case dangling from his opposite hand. He puts his typewriter on the stool, and leans his rifle against a wall. He pulls a large cigar from his vest, and spends the next few lines of dialogue trying unsuccessfully to light it with a Zippo.

MR. ALIGARI: How can you be here? I thought you were — [*Hesitates.*]

PAPA: What did you think I was?

MR. ALIGARI: Well, um um . . . God, I guess. That is, a lot of people I don't know thought you were. Still do, I would imagine. I've never really read —

PAPA: You have no wine? A *rioja*?

MR. ALIGARI: No, I haven't got a thing.

PAPA: Too many people haven't.

MR. ALIGARI: I don't even know where I am. Am I in Africa, now?

PAPA: I liked Africa. A man sees a new country and he likes it immoderately. He knows it is good. It is like a woman who accepts her man and his clean love. I liked the people and the land very much, but it is the land you learn to like first. Then you can begin to like the people. I liked Africa as soon as I woke up on my first cool morning in camp and had my first whisky. The first one is the best. I could fish and hunt there.

MR. ALIGARI: I always wanted to go to Africa. Or Norway.

PAPA: Every country is good. It is the men who make the country bad.

MR. ALIGARI: Is it good here?

LOUDSPEAKER: The time is exactly 11:14.

Papa puts his cigar back into his vest, followed by his Zippo. He goes to the blackboard and letters in large blocks: PAPA. Then he retrieves his rifle, readies it for firing, and stands as if looking across a plain.

LOUDSPEAKER: Bhwana! Look, the big cat! [*Papa aims the rifle.*] No, Bhwana, over there! [*Papa aims the rifle in the opposite direction.*] No, Bhwana, that is the car!

Papa takes off his glasses, leans the rifle against his leg, takes out a large khaki handkerchief and wipes his glasses, then puts them on. He looks out over the plain again, then up at the loudspeaker. Then he takes off his glasses and puts them in his vest pocket. He picks up the rifle and aims it at the loudspeaker.

LOUDSPEAKER: Ha ha ha ha ha.

Papa squeezes the trigger. There is a loud click. He squeezes it again and again. After each click there is a short burst of laughter from the loudspeaker. Papa drops the rifle to the floor and stands with his head down, carefully avoiding looking at Mr. Aligari, who is behind him.

LOUDSPEAKER: Bhwana! Look, the elephant!

Papa goes to the typewriter and sits on the stool with the typewriter on his lap. He takes a sheet of paper from his vest and puts it into the machine. He thinks for a while, then very slowly, with a great show of choosing the right key, taps it once.

LOUDSPEAKER: Dark laughter again, Bhwana.

Papa pulls the sheet of paper from the machine and puts it back into his vest pocket.

MR. ALIGARI: [*Quietly*] Too bad about the big cat.

PAPA: [*Still in character*] Tomorrow we will shoot again.

MR. ALIGARI: I'm sorry you didn't get him today.

PAPA: [*Breaking character, peevishly*] Ah, the shooting's lousy around here. A man alone doesn't have

a fucking chance. I shoulda stayed in India, for cat's
sake.

MR. ALIGARI: I always wanted to go to India.

*Papa walks to the door, dragging his rifle on the floor and
carrying his typewriter dangling from the opposite hand.*

MR. ALIGARI: [*Spanish*] Buenas tardes.

LOUDSPEAKER: [*After the door slams shut behind
Papa*] Buenas tardes.

*Resolutely, Mr. Aligari tries the door again but again finds
it locked. He walks restlessly around the room, glancing
expectantly at the door and at the loudspeaker. He stops in
front of the punching bag and starts to swing his fist at it,
but arrests his fist just before it would have made contact.
He walks to the stool and sits on it. He notices the lettering
on the blackboard and goes over and wipes it off. Then he
returns to the stool and sits on it.*

LOUDSPEAKER: Take a ten-minute smoke break.

MR. ALIGARI: [*Sarcastically*] Many thanks. [*He takes
out a cigarette and puts it into his mouth.*]

LOUDSPEAKER: No smoking, please.

*Mr. Aligari takes out his lighter and with a great show
of daring, looking up at the loudspeaker, prepares to light
his cigarette. A piercing siren noise comes from the loudspeaker. Mr. Aligari puts his lighter and cigarette away,
and the siren noise stops.*

MR. ALIGARI: Well, come on, let's get on with it.
[*Nothing happens.*] Come on, trot out your next
object lesson.

LOUDSPEAKER: No spitting.

MR. ALIGARI: Who's spitting?

LOUDSPEAKER: Keep off the grass.

MR. ALIGARI: There *is* no grass.

LOUDSPEAKER: No swimming beyond this point?

MR. ALIGARI: There *is* no point. [*He giggles.*]

LOUDSPEAKER: No passing in this lane. City bylaw.

MR. ALIGARI: Aw, shut up! [*More siren noise from the loudspeaker.*]

MR. ALIGARI: [*Yelling*] I'm sorry!

LOUDSPEAKER: Post no bills.

MR. ALIGARI: [*Despondently*] Do not feed the animals.

LOUDSPEAKER: No trespassing.

MR. ALIGARI: No fishing.

LOUDSPEAKER: No hunting.

MR. ALIGARI: No parking.

LOUDSPEAKER: No stop.

MR. ALIGARI: No sale.

LOUDSPEAKER: No dice.

MR. ALIGARI: No soap.

LOUDSPEAKER: No.

MR. ALIGARI: No.

LOUDSPEAKER: No.

MR. ALIGARI: No.

LOUDSPEAKER : No.

MR. ALIGARI: [*He pauses. Then he gets onto his feet and shouts*] Yes!

LOUDSPEAKER: No.

MR. ALIGARI: [*Louder*] Yessss!

Siren noise comes from the loudspeaker. The Man of Steel, The Sultan of Swat, and Papa come energetically into the room. They stand together, watching Mr. Aligari. The siren noise stops.

LOUDSPEAKER: The time is exactly 11:57.

Mr. Aligari goes to the blackboard, picks up chalk, and letters in large blocks: DANIEL ALIGARI. He looks at his wristwatch and letters: 4:30 PM. The four men look up at the loudspeaker. Silence lies heavily in the room. Finally:
  Mr. Aligari coughs.
  The Man of Steel coughs.
  Papa coughs.
  The Sultan of Swat coughs.

MR. ALIGARI: [*Looking at his watch*] 4:31 now.

THE SULTAN OF SWAT: 4:31.

PAPA: 4:31 is a good time.

THE MAN OF STEEL: They said it is 11:57.

THE SULTAN OF SWAT: But he says it is 4:31.

They are all looking at Mr. Aligari.

MR. ALIGARI: Standard time.

PAPA: It is good to have a standard time.

LOUDSPEAKER: You are all confined to barracks until further notice.

All of them except for Mr. Aligari start to leave.

MR. ALIGARI: Wait! [*They stop.*] Why don't you all wait right here? I am going to wait right here.

They all look at one another.

THE MAN OF STEEL: They said we are all confined to barracks.

MR. ALIGARI: I say why? Or how come? Why? Why don't you stick right here and see what happens?

PAPA: It never happens. Nothing happens. To you.

Mr. Aligari looks around the room, like a strategy-minded general reconnoitering a prospective battlefield.

MR. ALIGARI: Watch!

Mr. Aligari walks briskly over to the blackboard and rips it from the wall, where it had been attached by screws. He throws it onto the floor.

THE MAN OF STEEL: Oh!

PAPA: Oh!

THE SULTAN OF SWAT: Wow!

Mr. Aligari strides over to the punching bag, and after two or three efforts, rips it off its support and throws it to the floor.

THE MAN OF STEEL: Yes! [*He makes a gesture with his fist.*]

The Man of Steel walks over and kicks the punching bag.

THE SULTAN OF SWAT: Wowee!

The Sultan of Swat kicks the punching bag. Papa wordlessly stomps on the blackboard. A siren noise comes from the loudspeaker. Mr. Aligari picks up the stool by its legs and swings it against the loudspeaker until the loudspeaker is ripped from the wall and crashes to the floor. The siren noise is cut off abruptly by this action. The Man of Steel, Papa, and The Sultan of Swat walk over to the dead loudspeaker and look at it for a few moments, then turn away from it.

MR. ALIGARI: [*Puffing, hands on knees*] That's what happens.

THE SULTAN OF SWAT: Wowee!

PAPA: That was remarkable. True and remarkable.

THE MAN OF STEEL: Boy, oh boy! You know what you are?

MR. ALIGARI: [*Lifts his finger.*] Don't say it.

THE MAN OF STEEL: [*With a tone of wonder.*] You're a hero, that's what you are.

THE SULTAN OF SWAT: A little hero.

MR. ALIGARI: Nope. Nope. Nope, not a hero. Not me. I don't want anyone calling me a hero. Not me. Nope.

THE SULTAN OF SWAT: No, but that's what you are. Hero, hero, hero.

MR. ALIGARI: [*After a pause*] No, I'll tell you who's a hero. [*To the Sultan of Swat*] You, you are definitely a hero. [*The Sultan of Swat bows his head.*] [*To Papa*] You are a hero, big guy. [*Papa bows his head.*] [*To the Man of Steel*] You, you are a jeezly hero, man. [*The Man of Steel bows his head.*] See what I mean? You guys are a holy trinity of heroes.

THE MAN OF STEEL, PAPA, THE SULTAN OF SWAT: [*Together*] We are the heroes. Oh, boy!

MR. ALIGARI: You are confined to barracks. [*They start to go.*] Only kidding! [*They stop.*] I'm just a guy. I work at a desk in a candy factory. [*Pause*] Used to work at a desk in a candy factory.

THE SULTAN OF SWAT, PAPA, THE MAN OF STEEL: [*Together, heads bowed.*] Yum! A candy factory.

Mr. Aligari walks to the door, pauses, reaches for the door-knob, then drops his hand to his side. He looks around at the rubble. Then he puts his hand on the doorknob and wrenches the door crashing open. He looks at the open door for a moment. Then he takes a deep breath.

MR. ALIGARI: [*Leaving*] So long, heroes.

THE SULTAN OF SWAT, PAPA, THE MAN OF STEEL: [*Together, fairly loudly*] Yum!

CURTAIN.